"You have no questions, then." Zago watched her, telling himself he did not know why his chest was too tight, a sensation that did not make his gut feel any better about this woman and her masks and lies.

Unless it was the righteous fury of a brother avenging his sister, that was. And what else could it be? "I suppose it is an everyday occurrence for you, is it?"

"To be kidnapped?" Irinka shook her head, and he could remember the silk of her hair against his skin. Like a taunt. "This is my first time. I'll be certain to review the experience later with the authorities, but I don't really know that I could possibly predict what you might do, Zago." When her blue gaze met his then, it was direct. Not the least bit *airy*. "I was certain that after the last time we saw each other, you would never wish to lay eyes on me again."

KIDNAPPED FOR HIS REVENGE

CAITLIN CREWS

PRESENTS

**Harlequin®
PRESENTS™**

ISBN-13: 978-1-335-93974-6

Recycling programs
for this product may
not exist in your area.

Kidnapped for His Revenge

Harlequin Enterprises ULC
22 Adelaide St. West, 41st Floor
Toronto, Ontario M5H 4E3, Canada
www.Harlequin.com

Printed in Lithuania

MIX
Paper | Supporting
responsible forestry
FSC® C021394

USA TODAY bestselling, RITA® Award–nominated and critically acclaimed author **Caitlin Crews** has written more than one hundred and thirty books and counting. She has a master's and PhD in English literature, thinks everyone should read more category romance and is always available to discuss her beloved alpha heroes—just ask. She lives in the Pacific Northwest with her comic book–artist husband, is always planning her next trip and will never, ever read all the books in her to-be-read pile. Thank goodness.

Books by Caitlin Crews

Harlequin Presents

A Billion-Dollar Heir for Christmas
Wedding Night in the King's Bed
Her Venetian Secret
Forbidden Royal Vows
Greek's Christmas Heir

Innocent Stolen Brides

The Desert King's Kidnapped Virgin
The Spaniard's Last-Minute Wife

The Teras Wedding Challenge

A Tycoon Too Wild to Wed

The Diamond Club

Pregnant Princess Bride

Notorious Mediterranean Marriages

Greek's Enemy Bride
Carrying a Sicilian Secret

Visit the Author Profile page
at Harlequin.com for more titles.

To Voltron, now and forever.

CHAPTER ONE

As KIDNAPS WENT, Irinka Scott-Day thought hers was rather civilized.

The London weather was hideous, which was to say, typical for an April morning. Irinka had left her sweetheart of a house in Notting Hill in a rush that morning. Normally she liked to stop and admire the eclectic bright colors of the houses and doors along the Portobello Road where she lived—guaranteed to lift the spirits even in the midst of the worst of Britain's gray doldrums—but not today. She was not a person who was easily frazzled, and would not describe herself that way even now, but she had been out entirely too late the night before.

On the job, naturally. Irinka had given up dating sometime during her university years—

Well.

She had never *dated*, exactly. And she knew precisely when and why she'd given it up after that summer that she would also not describe as *dating*—because what an insipid word that was and how little it applied to those hot, breathless months—but there was no point thinking about the epic mistakes of the past.

Forget the past and lose an eye, but dwell on the past and lose both eyes, as her mother liked to say, claiming it was a Russian proverb though, possibly, it was her own bloodthirstiness.

But Irinka did not want to think about her mother. She loved Roksana dearly, but her mother was not what anyone would call a *soothing influence*.

When Irinka dashed outside, doing a great impression of *frazzled*, she'd expected the typical sullen clouds and grim drizzle and had dressed accordingly. She was not prepared for the rain to be heaving it down, bucketing into the streets so that the tired old roads were almost immediately swamped.

It was the bloody great puddles that did it, in the end.

Because she rushed outside expecting to make her way to Notting Hill Gate to either hail a black cab— because she was supernaturally capable of summoning cabs at will, an unimaginable feat in the press and clamor of Central London, especially when it was pissing it down—or take her chances on the Tube. But it was so wet that she paused at the curb outside her own brightly painted door, debating whether or not she ought to go and change the exquisite leather boots she was wearing, produced by the finest Italian craftsmen in a little-known Milanese shop because she liked an artisan, for her proper wellies.

She didn't notice the gleaming black SUV until

it was right there in front of her. Maybe it had been there all along, idling and waiting for her to emerge. It was hard to tell in the downpour and in any case, what she was focused on was the fact she was soaked where she stood.

"You look like you need a ride, ma'am," came a solicitous female voice, and the truth was that Irinka *did* need a ride.

All she saw was the black vehicle, and perhaps her need of it, and so she gratefully climbed inside, expecting it to be a minicab or an Uber or the like. It didn't surprise her at all that one should simply *appear* because she needed it. It was her single magical trick, after all. She settled back, sighing a little at the inescapable fact that magic or no magic, she was sopping wet after standing outside all of ten seconds.

Then the SUV started moving. And the locks engaged, a soft but insistent *click*.

Her intuition kicked in, sending a little jolt down her spine.

There were no licenses on display on the console and as she looked for them, an interior window went up and created a barrier between her and the driver. She had the urge to try the door handle nearest her, but restrained herself.

Because if Irinka knew one thing in this life, it was that the appearance of unconcern and ease—or of sheer indifference, whatever worked—was often the only weapon required in most situations.

So she folded her hands, gazed serenely out the

window, and made herself wait as the vehicle that was very obviously not a taxi of any kind made its way out of Central London and was soon enough on a motorway, heading away from the city.

That was worrisome.

This was when she decided that she was, in fact, being kidnapped.

Irinka considered pulling out her mobile and texting an SOS to her best friends, who also happened to be her business partners. But what could they do other than make calls that might or might not help when she had no identifying features of the vehicle to share and didn't know where they were headed? Together, she and her friends ran His Girl Friday, an agency of requirement, as Irinka liked to call it. They catered toward unconventional solutions to certain problems for the very wealthy. A niche market, perhaps. Luckily enough, there was no shortage of wealthy people with entirely too much money on their hands, happy to outsource whenever possible.

Irinka and her friends had found an opportunity, gone after it, and made it theirs.

They had all gone to university together. Lynna cooked for tremendously wealthy people who liked to have gourmet meals on call. Auggie was the queen of PR, rescuing the reputations of those who probably didn't deserve it, but could certainly afford it. Maude was something of a forest creature, which was helpful as she did groundskeeping on grand old estates and made the ancient gardens she found there nothing short of enchanted.

Irinka's contribution was the one they never advertised. What she did was only whispered about in certain exalted circles. Word of mouth was the only way that a particular sort of wealthy man with a specific, thorny problem knew to reach out to her—or would consider doing so in the first place. Because otherwise, she simply looked like the typical bored heiress like so many of the girls she'd known her whole life, made up of pedigrees and impressive parentage, some fame and some notoriety. All of them kicking around the Big Smoke, marking time while they waited for the various trust funds and inheritances to kick in.

To the outside world, Irinka was merely the secretary of His Girl Friday, general dogsbody, and office manager. And she wasn't half bad at those things— she considered herself a dab hand at a spreadsheet, as it happened—but the truth was that really, the office didn't need much managing or secretarial support. The four of them did more work in their group chat than many of the billionaires Irinka had spent time with did in the course of their endless board meetings and tedious rolling phone calls.

The truth was, first, that she had no trust funds or incoming grand inheritances. She was not an heiress, not in the way that people assumed she was. She was, through no fault of her own, the infamous illegitimate daughter of an extremely high-in-the-instep duke, however. That was a fact. And it was true that he had settled something of a fortune upon her in the hopes that she would go away.

There are fortunes and then there are dukedoms, Roksana had said dismissively when the papers had all screeched to the world the settlement details she'd won for her daughter in court. *Trust a duke to throw a few crumbs and pretend it's a castle.*

That was what happened when a stodgy old duke had an illicit affair with an extremely spiteful Russian supermodel—the mononymous Roksana, beloved in all fashion circles as much for her cutting remarks as for the vicious blades of her cheekbones—and then imagined that he could walk away from her and face no repercussions.

It had taken a great deal of tabloid attention and several court cases to not only prove Irinka's paternity beyond any legal or biological doubt, but to force the Duke to provide for her in a comparable fashion to the way he provided for the children he'd had with his long-suffering blue-blooded wife. Irinka had thus learned early on that the best way to get men to do what she wanted was to smile prettily, threaten vaguely, and invoke her mother's name whenever necessary.

She had been a fixture of the society pages since she was a teenager, sometimes because she sought attention and sometimes because she couldn't escape it. That was when she'd learned that people—sometimes a whole lot of people—preferred the idea of her to the reality of her, at least according to the sneering press. Irinka had adjusted accordingly, and had become mysterious. This was useful when she was at the same absurd functions that her legitimate half siblings attended, where they could all bare their teeth at each other and try to outdo one another's level of icy, vicious courtesy—and then Irinka would disappear.

It was one of Irinka's favorite games, if she was honest. They were mean, she was mysterious, and this was how her reputation was built.

And it was important that she kept it up even now that she was older and supposedly wiser on this side of her university days, because it was important that most of the largely inbred European society viewed her with the same vague mix of distaste and weaponized pity that her half siblings did. Oh, sure, it was buried under jolly laughter and endless invitations to this party or that. But at the end of the day they would all whisper behind their hands that it was *lucky* Irinka was so pretty, because there was certain to be someone blue-blooded and broke—or cluelessly American—who would be more than happy to take her on.

Eventually.

But it would never make her anything but the discarded by-blow of a duke. In those circles, that was still a stain.

And the sort of pitiable, socially questionable creature Irinka was widely held to be by a certain strata of high society could be expected to do no better than to maintain a pointless secretarial job with her

university mates, waiting for her pedigreed prince—
or some nouveau riche Wall Street banker, the more
likely bet—to arrive.

The reality was that Irinka had learned early in life
that it was best to hide in plain sight. In fact, she'd
become an expert at it.

And that was why some of the wealthiest men in
the world hired her. They could count on her dis-
cretion, because she was excellent at disguises. Not
only her appearance, but her voice, adopting any accent she pleased. She could change her mannerisms
and even how she held her body, so that even people
who knew her would not recognize her if she didn't
want them to.

She had become the most sought-after breakup
artist in Europe.

Irinka was the one who appeared when a man
needed to end a relationship and needed to make certain that there would be no attempts on the part of the
woman that he was scraping off to chase after him,
begging for second thoughts and third chances. She
had played wounded wives and furious girlfriends, as
well as slinky other women, too many times to count.

Sometimes she was the woman at the bar who the
man in question couldn't seem to look away from, in-
furiating his date into losing his number. Sometimes
she walked into hotel rooms, "surprising" an intimate
scene. Sometimes she arranged herself in a bed in
the same hotel rooms, claiming to be the significant

other who'd come as a surprise and who, pray, was the woman on her man's arm?

Being so good at these performances of hers was a great way to drum up business.

What it was not, she reflected as the SUV drove on, taking her farther and farther away from London, was a decent way to make sure she had no enemies.

All the ways and whys a person might take against a woman who did the job she did clattered about in her head as she sat there, locked up tight in the back seat. She kept gazing out the window, looking as if, perhaps, she might have lapsed off into a spot of meditation. Or so she hoped.

But she was not entirely surprised to find that when the SUV turned off the motorway, it was to head toward a private airfield.

Truthfully, it was not *completely* unexpected that someone might wish to kidnap her. It did not *beggar belief* that she might have upset a person to this degree.

Irinka supposed that meant she lived a life of drama, the very sort Roksana had lived, still lived, and always warned her daughter to avoid. In dark and dramatic tones. But it was significantly less dramatic than her childhood, which had involved being chased by paparazzi and fielding abuse hurled at her on the streets by those who took umbrage against her mother's tactics and temerity.

Really, a pleasant ride in the back of a lovely vehicle and the prospect of a plane ride was a bit of a holiday compared to all that.

But in an abundance of caution, she took her mobile and stuffed it into her boot, where it pressed against her shin and was not exactly comfortable— but was less likely to be confiscated straight off. Then she waited as serenely as possible as the SUV drove straight out onto the tarmac and pulled up next to a waiting jet.

The window went down between her and her driver and the woman looked back through the rearview mirror with a particular, assessing sort of look that told Irinka many things. Most importantly, that this woman worked for someone else. She had that look of smooth, hired muscle. There was that blankness around the eyes.

Not, in other words, the person she really had to worry about. Not the person engineering this. So there was really no point attempting to extricate herself, because a look at the woman made it clear that she would suppress all such efforts. And quickly.

"Are you going to walk onto that plane or am I going to have to carry you?" the woman asked.

A glance at her biceps made Irinka believed that she could do this. And without much difficulty.

"Are those my only options?" Irinka asked, languidly. "Because I was headed to the spa. This does seem like rather an interruption."

The woman didn't laugh. She didn't really respond at all. She just continued to stare, dead-eyed, through the rearview mirror and it occurred to Irinka that perhaps she should be slightly more concerned than she was. That this was becoming less of a lark and more of a problem by the moment.

She wasn't sure that hysterics would work, however, which was a pity. She was excellent at hysterics. She could turn them on and off, complete with tears, at will and often did. "May I ask where I'm going?" she asked brightly. "I do hope it's a holiday. It's exhausting to be kidnapped. I'm afraid I'm going to need quite a bit of recovery."

"My employer will explain everything to you when you arrive in Italy," the woman told her.

"Amo l'Italia!" Irinka cried. Theatrically. "How I long to gaze upon the waters of Lake Como. Or wander the ruins of so many centuries of civilization in the Eternal City, *la bella Roma*. Or *immerse myself* in the grandeur of Firenze's art and culture—"

"You are going to Venice," the driver said curtly.

Venice.

Irinka felt the usual deep lurch inside of her that she always did when she heard the name of that city, but she shoved it aside. She inclined her head in acquiescence and the woman got out of the vehicle, then opened her door. Irinka climbed out, not sure if she was happy or offended that the rain had settled down to a faint mist. Sheets of rain might have helped now. At least, where her mood was concerned.

As she stood there, contemplating the vagaries of the weather, the woman held out her hand. It was not an encouraging sort of gesture. Not from this tall, muscled woman who looked like she ate Cross-Fit gyms for breakfast.

"Your bag, please," the woman said.

"A girl doesn't simply hand over her purse to any passing ruffian." Irinka laughed as if this was a cocktail party, not a kidnapping. "Have you done this before? I think if you had, you would know that."

She stared back, impassive. "Your bag, please."

"Are you going to hurt me?" she asked.

The woman frowned, but only slightly. "My orders are to deliver you safely to your final destination. But I will do what is necessary to achieve my objectives."

"Noted." Irinka handed over her bag. And was immediately glad that she'd moved her mobile when she rifled through it, then handed it back.

"Empty your pockets," the woman said.

Irinka made a show of producing her empty coat pockets for review, but shrunk back when she moved too close. "This is a Burberry," she said with a bit of a shriek, as if the other woman's proximity was an assault. "It is to be *gently handled* with *respect* and *reverence*."

At that, the woman actually sighed in exasperation and Irinka felt a bit of relief wash right through her.

Because exasperation was a human reaction. An assassin wouldn't crack, but someone's security detail might. Only a little, sure. But it made Irinka significantly more convinced that violence wasn't the objective here.

Before the woman could ask, she unzipped her coat and patted each of her pockets on the skinny jeans she wore tucked into her poor, sodden boots.

"I don't know what you're looking for, but I am not packing explosives on my person. Isn't that what airport security is worried about?"

"Let's go," muttered her captor, and then Irinka was being escorted up the steps and onto the waiting jet.

Once inside, she took a look around, noting all the details and flourishes that indicated that this was a high-end jet. And not the sort that was normally rented out. There were personal touches here. She had flown all over the world on private jets, for work and pleasure. She could tell the difference.

The moment she boarded, she shared a bright, fake smile with a waiting flight attendant, and asked for the bathroom. Once inside, she pulled out her mobile and typed a quick text to her friends.

Looks like I'm going on a bit of an unexpected holiday, she told them. *If you don't hear from me in three days, initiate the emergency protocol.*

I'm sorry, "the emergency protocol?" Auggie replied almost at once. *That's all you're going to say? No details? You must be joking.*

There is a bit of a time crunch, Irinka typed back. *Just track my mobile. You know you do anyway.*

I thought you said that no one would dare do anything to you any longer, Lynna responded. *That your reputation precedes you and even the billionaire class is helpless before your power, or something.*

This might be a case of my reputation preceding me, now that you mention it, Irinka replied. *I don't feel that I'm in danger. Not yet.*

Thank you, replied Maude. *That's not at all concerning.*

But Irinka didn't dare take any more time in the bathroom. She didn't want to invite anyone to come crashing back in. She slid her mobile back into her boot, wiggling her leg so that it went down and rested snugly against one calf. She eyed the boot critically, now that she wasn't being observed. The leather was supple but had its own structural integrity, so the fact that she'd chucked something down there wasn't obvious.

You must spoil before you spin, Roksana always muttered. Practice might not make perfect here, but it was working.

Irinka flushed so that her captors would hear it, then washed her hands and checked her appearance automatically. That was what her mother had always taught her to do.

Beauty is a commodity, Roksana had always told her, with the intensity she reserved for life lessons. *That makes it a weapon. And you must always make certain your blade is sharp.*

Irinka smoothed her hair slightly and fixed what she could of her face with only a bit of water in the mirror.

Then she sailed back out to find the flight attendant waiting for her, beckoning her to a seat. Of course, they took her coat, politely. And, of course, she saw Ms. Thug herself sitting opposite her seat, and tracked the way she swept her gaze all over Irinka now that there was no coat to block the view.

Irinka was braced for the woman to call out the mobile in her boot, but she didn't. So Irinka sat down in the seat they'd designated, buckled herself in, and smiled widely as the plane began to taxi.

"This is very exciting," she said. "I do love surprises. Will there be snacks?"

Once again, she saw exasperation move all over the woman's face, mixed with the slightest bit of something almost dazed. As if she couldn't believe that Irinka was reacting this way and didn't quite know what to do about it.

Excellent, Irinka thought.

Because she'd made quite a study of reading people in her lifetime. Initially because it was necessary. There were her mother's many lovers, a fact of life Irinka supposed she'd gotten used to before she'd even entered the world. Since Roksana had married pretty quickly after her relationship with the Duke deteriorated, to great tabloid furor. Whether her temporary husband had at any point believed that the baby Roksana carried was his was unknown. Either way, Roksana had wasted no time divorcing him after Irinka was born.

Roksana had bestowed the Duke's surname upon

their daughter as a shot across the bow. A warning and a proclamation, despite his rages. And Irinka had kept the name all this time, long after Roksana had decided that the Duke—having paid up—was beneath her notice, out of spite.

Later she'd learned how to read the Duke himself, her ever-indignant biological father, on the few-and-far-between occasions she'd met with him, providing him a receptacle for his enduring outrage that his actions had indeed had consequences. She could read her unfriendly siblings, two half brothers and one half sister, from across ballrooms and knew without ever having to discuss it that they were all *filled with umbrage* over the fact that Irinka got all the attention.

Later, this ability of hers had become the foundation of her job.

Because, of course, there were her clients. She could read them easily. The bulk of them were repeat customers because they much preferred it when she handled the unpleasantness of the end of their love affairs. So she knew things about them that perhaps only their ex-lovers did.

It was almost intimate.

A lot like being kidnapped, it turned out. Irinka felt confident now that Ms. Thug wasn't going to hurt her. Or really do anything but deliver her, like a parcel.

That was comforting enough as long as Irinka stayed in the moment and didn't think too much about the future.

The plane took off. Snacks were, in fact, provided.

And as the plane rose into the air, leaving the thick, dark clouds of England behind, she tried to think of who she knew in Venice.

It was difficult, as the sort of men she worked for had properties everywhere. Any one of them could have a property in Venice. Many of them were unaware of how many properties they actually had, as that was the province of the money people they employed, who talked endlessly about *portfolios* and were absentee landlords.

Irinka began to wonder how much of her bravado was actually shock as it began to wear off.

The truth was, civil or not, she'd been flown off to God knows where and although no one had hurt her, she thought it had been very clear that if necessary, the blank-eyed woman across from her would have manhandled her onto this plane.

Woman-handled, she corrected herself.

And it was a lot like how she operated in the world, now that she thought about it. The threat was always implied. It didn't have to be explicit.

It turned out it was far more unpleasant than she realized. She would have to make a mental note.

Then again, maybe the threat was Venice. Maybe that was the only threat that worked.

Soon enough the plane began its descent. Once they landed into the blues and deep greens of Italy, Irinka was gently encouraged to get into yet another car. This one drove her to a dock, where it was suggested that she get into a boat.

By this point, the only languid thing about her was the smile she kept on her face the whole time, because she knew that people who wanted her intimidated found it irritating. She'd been told so often enough.

She made herself sit bonelessly. She fairly lounged on her seat in the little jet boat as it chugged along, took a turn, and then there they were. On the Grand Canal in Venice, the city of mystery.

And memory.

Irinka had only been here once before. That summer directly after university when she had discovered, once and for all, that recklessness and heedlessness—and being *seen* and *known*—were not for her.

She was not nostalgic. She refused to let those memories pull at her. But she felt tendrils all the same—whispers in the dark that she'd thought she'd extinguished. Scraps of touch, of heat—

Nothing that needed to be dug up again, she told herself briskly. No one liked the dead coming back to life.

And so she was already feeling something like bittersweet, and something a good deal darker than nostalgia, when the boat began to slow. She looked up and it took considerable effort to school her expression.

Because she knew the house they were approaching. Not that it was a *house*.

It was one of Venice's oldest palazzos, set back from the Grand Canal with a garden in between, thanks to a fire in some bygone century that had turned its fifteenth-century facade to ash. What remained was a lovely old house that managed to convey the same air of genteel exhaustion as the rest of the city, having long since been repaired and renovated.

Her heart picked up in her chest. She could feel the effect of this place, everywhere, and the thudding of the blood in her veins made it remarkably difficult to smile serenely at her captors as they docked the boat and then waited for her to climb out.

But she did it.

No matter what dead things were rising here, most notably inside her.

And she could pretend that she'd heard dire things about the brackish water in Venetian canals. She could pretend that she was worried about all the other boats and how easy it would be to be swept up and run down while splashing around out there.

But that wasn't why she didn't turn and run, then swim for it.

It was the same thing it had always been. That deep and unfortunate pull that dragged her here whether she wanted to come or not.

That madness she had only ever experienced once before.

She told herself that this time it was nothing but curiosity.

It was warmer in Venice. Brighter, though still the skies were a touch moody. She followed where she was led—because she had to know, now—marching up the central pathway that led to the grand front entrance of the palazzo.

With every step, it wasn't just her heart that reacted but every other part of her. She could feel a tightness in her throat as if there were still words unsaid when she knew better. She could feel her chest constrict as if she would finally let herself sob, but she refused.

She still refused.

And then it all seemed to be happening too quickly. She was marched inside, into dim, grand rooms. She was ushered through the palazzo's high-ceilinged, exquisitely wrought spaces that flowed one into another, up the stairs from the water line, and then into what she knew too well was the main living area on the second floor.

She was delivered inside, the door was closed behind her, and then...

There he was.

He stood out on one of the balconies, a study in male elegance. He did not turn to look at her, but Irinka had no doubt whatsoever that he knew she was there.

She supposed that he was probably drawing out the tension of this moment, but she was grateful for it.

Because she had never intended to lay eyes on him again. And she wasn't prepared now.

He was looking out toward the canal and she understood with a sort of *winnowing* sensation inside her that he'd watched her approach.

Irinka tried to make sense of what was happening instead of simply *reacting* to it. Why, years later, would he go to the trouble of having her picked up off the London street and transported across Europe? Why now? What could he want?

But she refused to ask.

And her brain refused to cooperate, anyway. All it wanted to do was dig up old graves and let the ghosts dance free.

He took his time straightening. And, for a moment, she was staring at the long, finely molded line of his back. His shoulders were wide, his waist narrow. Everything he wore was exquisite, tailored specifically to his body and his preferences. And so while all he appeared to be wearing was a shirt and trousers, the effect was mouthwatering.

It turned out she was still susceptible to him. This was not information she'd wanted to learn.

Even with his back to her, everything about him was ferociously masculine and astonishingly sophisticated. She had seen so many men who should have been like him in the years since. All of these wealthy, powerful men, who were somehow incapable of sorting out their own relationships.

It only occurred to her now that perhaps her excellence in her profession had been her way of trying to convince herself that he was just like all of them.

But he wasn't.

He turned, then, and it was as if he'd thrown open windows in a dark room and let the morning light in.

Because there was no one like this man.

There never had been. They never would be.

His back was poetry rendered in finely muscled male flesh. She knew that already. But looking at him, face-to-face after all this time, she found herself unprepared for the impact of him. Memory had dulled the sheer brutal thrust of his beauty.

Or perhaps time had honed it.

If Irinka's beauty was a weapon she'd been taught to wield, his was something else entirely. Looking at him was like stepping into an ancient cathedral, like the very famous one not far from his palazzo. It was an experience of soaring, everything drawn up into the force of him by something outside human comprehension.

His hair was dark and close-cropped. His eyes looked black. He was sculpted to perfection, formed by generations of beautiful Venetian men, tall and dark-haired and with flashing eyes, and the stunning women they had married as if it was no more than their due.

She had studied all of them in the portraits that hung on the walls in this place, sitting cheek by jowl with Picassos, Caravaggios, and Titians.

Irinka told herself that she was deliberately standing still, her head up and her eyes on him. But the truth was that she felt frozen into place.

She felt his eyes all over her the way his hands had been, once. The way his mouth had followed, teaching her complicated lessons about immolation.

And she didn't know why he had brought her here.

But that hardly mattered. Because she wasn't the girl she'd been that summer. She never had been before, and never had been since. That was the important thing.

So she smiled her patented languid smile, the one she hadn't perfected yet when she'd been here last. And she tilted her head to the side as she regarded him, as if he was the captured animal in the zoo here, not her.

"Hello, Zago," she said, and she hadn't said his name in so long that she could taste it on her tongue, rich and decadent. "What an extraordinary invitation. I've never received one quite like it. Your standards must be slipping."

But Zago Baldissera only smiled, sending a dark shiver down the length of her spine.

"It was not an invitation," he replied, in that voice that she understood, now, had haunted her all these years. In her dreams, just out of reach. "That time is long past. What you are here for is a reckoning."

CHAPTER TWO

ZAGO BALDISSERA HAD waited a long time for this moment.

Irinka Scott-Day, out of her element. Back here in this palazzo as if there had been no time at all between that fateful summer and now. As if that handful of years—that he could remember living through all too well—had been a blank, after all.

It felt like a *victory*.

And yet he never would have engineered this moment into being, however, had it not been for his sister.

He reminded himself that Nicolosa was the point of this. That it was Nicolosa, who had been crying for the last month straight, who deserved that revenge be taken in her name.

As her older brother and protector, he would have done what was necessary no matter what. It was simply a stroke of good luck that when he'd gone digging into the individuals who had been involved in his sister's heartbreak, he'd found Irinka.

Of all people.

He was tempted to consider it fate.

Hers, that was.

"A reckoning?"

Irinka drifted farther into the room, looking utterly unconcerned. This was the Palazzo delle Sospira. Even if it burned, and it had, it did not change. And his role in life was to make certain it never did. To fight as best he could to preserve the history and legacy of his family until the palazzo sank beneath the waters of the lagoon, as they all would, in time.

That eventuality came closer every day, but Zago thought of himself as a man who straddled time. It took, it gave, and he did what he must in between.

And what he needed to do today was this.

"Does the idea of a reckoning frighten you?" he asked when she seemed content enough to do nothing more than drift from a statue some claimed was an unknown Donatello liberated from Florence in the 1400s, to the Murano glass bowls on a side table, to the small figurines his great-grandmother had collected, all made for her by well-regarded artists of the time. "I suppose it should. Where would you even begin to tally up your sins? Do you even know *which* sin it is that I feel requires your penance, or do they all blend together?"

"I'm sure you have a laundry list."

She didn't sound *bored*, exactly. But, of course, she was too good at what she did for that.

Zago had spent the last month learning everything there was to know about this baffling creature that

Irinka had become. There had been nothing but glow-ing reviews from the otherwise extraordinarily picky and private men that he'd contacted under the guise of seeking the sort of woman who would do the kind of job for him that had been done to his sister.

He had found nothing but rapturous praise and he'd had to read between the lines. She was entirely professional. *Cold straight through,* one man had said admiringly. *All business.* Scenarios were discussed, then at least two top picks were selected in the event that circumstances required a change midstream. The date was picked out and agreed upon.

And then Irinka would appear—looking nothing like herself but still very much like a woman the man in question might actually be involved with, a critical detail—and would then do what needed to be done.

And the thing about her is that she's good at it, an-other man had confided. *A proper actress, in the end. Absolutely sells the scene and never the* same *scene twice. She is a national treasure.*

Zago intended to tarnish this treasure.

Or possibly wreck it entirely. He had yet to decide how this would go. It rather depended on her.

He watched as Irinka found a seat and then sank into it, looking entirely at her ease.

And the trouble was, even though he'd braced him-self, he really hadn't been prepared for that same elec-tric shock that he'd always felt in her presence. He wasn't prepared to find her even more compelling than he had three years ago.

He would have told himself that was impossible.

She looked as if she inhabited her body more now than she had then. As if every part of her was fully controlled, and he couldn't help but find that attractive. More than attractive. But then, she had always been beautiful. He had thought it the least interesting thing about her, in the end, but there was no denying it. No pretending that she was not her famously stunning mother's daughter in every regard.

In *every* regard, he reminded himself.

Irinka's thick black hair was clipped back at her nape, the long tail of it flipped over one shoulder. Her eyes were that blue that he'd liked to tell himself, in retrospect, were nothing but icy and cold, but they never had been. Not really. And they weren't now.

The only blue he had ever seen to compare was the water of Venice at dawn, mysterious and inviting.

He needed to vanquish the part of him that allowed her to haunt him even here, in this place where his ancestors had been traced to the ninth century, in one form or another.

Perhaps what he needed to do was dwell on the person she'd decided to become after leaving him. Because it was difficult not to assume that a woman who was that good at putting on all her different masks had put one on for him, too.

Maybe this squalid thing she did was who she really was. And maybe she had done it to him first.

A truth that sat unpleasantly in his gut.

"You have no questions, then." Zago watched her,

telling himself he did not know why his chest was too tight, a sensation that did not make his gut feel any better about this woman and her masks and lies. Unless it was the righteous fury of a brother avenging his sister, that was. And what else could it be? "I suppose it is an everyday occurrence for you, is it?"

"To be kidnapped?" Irinka shook her head, and he could remember the silk of her hair against his skin. Like a taunt. "This is my first time. I'll be certain to review the experience later with the authorities, but I don't really know that I could possibly predict what you might do, Zago." When her blue gaze met his, then, it was direct. Not the least bit *airy*. "I was certain that after the last time we saw each other, you would never wish to lay eyes on me again."

That was an alarmingly reductive take on what had happened between them, but he supposed that was the point. He had no intention of wading into her take on that mess of a summer. Zago doubted very much that he would be impressed with the spin she'd put on it.

Particularly because she had snuck out in the night like some kind of thief and had never looked back.

He refused to give her the satisfaction of bringing any of that up.

It would give the impression that he had held on to all of it, and he had not.

He had *not*.

"Indeed, I did not wish to see you again," he agreed. "Or even think of you, Irinka. You cannot imagine how little I wish these measures were necessary."

She smiled again, as if he had said something droll and amusing at the sort of cocktail parties that wearied him. Then she waved her hand, taking in the room all around them. The frescoed walls, antiques dating back to any number of fallen empires, and the Grand Canal beyond, whispering its silken threats and seductive invitations as it went. That it had taken so many, that it would take them all, that this was no more than the price of beauty in so small a life.

He normally found this comforting.

Or, at the very least, a commentary on the sort of pressure a Baldissera heir must be prepared to withstand as long as he—and the family legacy, embodied in this palazzo—stayed above the waterline. His life's work was to make certain he did.

There was less solace in it today, he found. He blamed Irinka for that, too.

"I assume you are meandering about in the direction of telling me why I am here?" she asked, though she did not sound as worried about that as he'd expected. As, perhaps, he'd wanted. If anything, she sounded like all that blue blood in her veins had finally taken hold and frozen her as solid as the country she came from. "The palazzo is looking lovely. You're maintaining it beautifully. I'm sure that your father would be proud."

And he was glad she'd said that. *Fiercely* glad.

Because she was reminding him, in the most subtle way possible—another hallmark of the way she did her dirty business, he'd been given to understand—

that she was not afraid to use the weapons she had. So there was no need for *him* to hold back, either.

His father had been absolutely certain that no one, living or dead, could care more for the palazzo and the Baldissera name than himself. He had died of heart failure when Zago was twenty-eight. And Zago had still been reeling from that loss, and from the mess it had been to excavate all of his father's secrets and plans and mistakes, a year later when he'd met Irinka.

He had shared too much with her and he had regretted it ever since.

But today it was a gift.

Because she was reminding him that there was no need to play nicely.

"You have a very interesting line of business, do you not?" Zago moved farther into the room and seated himself opposite her. He could have called for his staff to bring refreshments, but this wasn't a social visit and there was no need to worry about her comfort.

This was business. Family business.

"I do," she agreed, in that same pleasant tone with a whole *dukedom* of not-quite-expressed disdain beneath.

Zago could see why so many of her clients, who worked for their money—or at least had, once—and were easily bewitched by crumbling old ruins and the odd castle, were enamored of her. She was likely the only woman they ever encountered who quietly asserted the fact that she was *better* than them. Then refused to sleep with them, by all accounts.

They loved her for it.

He, personally, did not care to speculate about who she did or did not sleep with.

"I'm sure you remember me talking about my friends from university," she was saying, another dangerous nod toward their past. Because remembering anything could mean remembering everything, and he doubted she wanted that.

It occurred to him, then, that she was trying to minimize it—and there would be no need to do that if it wasn't as large and unwieldy a memory for her as it was for him, would there?

He told himself what he felt at that thought was mere interest, nothing more. It was *interesting*, that was all.

And she was still talking, chattering as if they were acquaintances at a brunch, the sort of event Zago would never attend. "We started a specialty sort of agency. My friends go off into the world and provide services for wealthy individuals who require them. One is a world-class chef. Another can pretty much fix any reputation, no matter what. Another one can take any family pile and transform it into a garden oasis. These are all very specialized skills. Meanwhile, I hold down the fort in our office."

Zago studied her lovely face for a long moment, but she seemed prepared to gaze back at him like that forever. Guileless. At her ease.

Deceitful to her core.

"That will be the last lie you tell me, Irinka," he said, with enough quiet fury that he saw her sit a little bit straighter. "Do you understand me? I know perfectly well you are not a receptionist."

"I'm an excellent receptionist."

"I'm more interested in your other pursuits." He settled back in his seat and told himself his heart beat faster only with the thrill of this chase reaching its end. There could be no other reason. "For example, I believe you are familiar with a certain Peruvian financier. Felipe De Osma."

She looked wholly unbothered by this line of questioning, but he didn't believe that, either. Surely it was her job to look unconcerned, and she was clearly an excellent actress. "Of course. He has contracted the services of our agency many times."

"And what services does he require of you?"

Her smile never wavered. "I'm afraid that the one thing we promise our clientele above all else is privacy. I can't tell you what it is we do for him or anyone else we may or may not do work for. Just as, if you were our client, I wouldn't tell anyone what we did for you, either."

Zago studied her. "I already know what you do."

She shrugged, and it made her hair move while another memory scraped over him. "How marvelous. Then I don't need to feel all *cloak and dagger* that I'm not telling you."

"Tell me about the events of about a month ago,"

he invited her. Though it was more of an order. "You walked into the luxury flat of Felipe De Osma despite the security measures in place, found him in a compromising position with a woman, and threw a glass of wine in his face." He thought he saw a trace of amusement in her blue eyes, but it was gone in a flash. "While he was mopping himself up, you launched into a spate of blistering, outraged Spanish, claiming that you were his lover. Are you?"

"What an indelicate question." But her eyes gleamed. "Even if it was remotely your concern, which it isn't, I can't imagine why I would answer you."

It was his turn to very obliquely look around the room, as if measuring the thickness of the walls and therefore the parameters of her cell here. "I'm certain I can convince you that it's in your best interest."

"I'm sure you think you can," Irinka said, which was not quite agreement. "What I'm more interested in is how you know what was said in the middle of an altercation in someone else's flat. Are you stalking Felipe? Whatever for?"

"I am not stalking anyone."

"Oh." And her expression was innocent enough, though Zago could see that gleam in her gaze intensify. "Do you outsource that the way you do kidnappers?"

And it didn't help to see that spark in her. To remember how he had ignited it and where it had taken them. Just as it did not help anything to find that he was not nearly as immune to her as he had expected he would be.

After all, he had offered her the world, and she had turned him down flat.

What was there to be susceptible to after that?

Especially when her behavior since proved that really, she had done him a favor.

Irinka kept her gaze trained on him, as if she could read him too easily. There was a part of him that was very much worried that she could.

But he told himself that was unlikely. "Speaking of outsourcing, how often do you go about interfering in other people's relationships and making women you don't even know cry?" he asked instead.

The strangest expression moved over her face then, and he told himself that it was an improvement, anyway, from her attempts at innocence. Whatever it was, it was more *real*. He was sure of it—even though it disappeared almost as quickly as it came.

"I'm sure I don't know what you mean."

"What I mean, Irinka, is that you are widely known as the breakup artist that every man of a certain sort needs on speed dial. If a man doesn't have the stomach to handle his own mess, you come and do it for him. Are you pretending that you don't? What other reason would you have for storming into Felipe De Osma's flat and disrupting the intimate evening he was having with another woman?"

"I still don't know what you're talking about."

"I wonder what would happen to your business if

I were to have a frank and far-reaching discussion with, say, a selection of tabloids about what it is you actually do at that agency of yours." He settled back against the ancient settee and gazed at the frescoed ceiling. "I can't help but notice that you've taken a great deal of trouble to make yourself seem toothless. Unremarkable. Everyone thinks of you as little more than a dilettante, wafting around Europe and pretending that you're some kind of party girl, when everyone knows that your father—*His Grace*—wants nothing to do with you. That must be painful." He watched her lift her chin a bit at that, as if it was a blow that landed. And he told himself that the searing sensation that moved through him then was a triumph. "Perhaps it is unsurprising that you choose to translate that kind of pain into preying on others. That is the sort of thing that rolls downhill, does it not?"

"That's a bit rich coming from the hereditary heir to an ancient Venetian fortune that was not exactly built on good vibes and sunshine, as I recall."

That was also a blow that landed. Zago didn't like it.

The truth, as far as he knew, was that no family that could trace itself into antiquity and yet still hold on tight to some of its spoils—like the palazzo they sat in now—could do so without what his father had always referred to as *uno brutto momento*. A bad moment.

In a family like theirs, there had been many. Some matched up with the wars that had made and destroyed and remade Europe. Some were of their own, personal making. Zago could remember his father's rants all throughout his childhood, increasing in intensity as the years went by, as if he could reach back through time and lecture his ancestors on the duties and legacies they had periodically neglected.

We must be the paragons our bloodline needs in the future to make up for the past, his father had liked to say in his later years, usually when Zago had dared interrupt him in his study. The place he liked to go to hide away from the world in general and his children in particular, leaving them to their own devices.

Sometimes Zago thought that he had been raised as a ghost, left to haunt the halls of the palazzo with all the rest.

He deeply regretted telling Irinka these things over the course of that summer.

And he could not forgive himself for trusting her with the stories—good and bad—of those who had come before him, not to mention with his father's obsessions.

He abandoned you, she had said once. *Without committing to actually leaving. That's quite a feat.*

And then she had abandoned him, too. But she had also made sure to leave, just to make sure that knife was stuck in deep. Zago thought he could feel it still, buried deep between his shoulder blades.

"The choice is yours," he told her now, and absolutely did not shift his position to relieve the bite of a knife that wasn't there.

He had long since decided that the burdens his father had bequeathed to him—like the weight of this palazzo and its history and the legacy that he was expected to tend and nurture into a future that expanded far beyond him, to say nothing of his family's ancient reputation all the social expectations that went with that in certain quarters of this country—were a gift.

No one ever said a gift had to *feel* good all the time.

A distinction he intended to make clear to Irinka this time around.

"A choice?" Irinka said that with mock delight and no little astonishment. "Am I truly being offered a choice? That's the first time all day."

He opted to ignore that. "The choice is very simple. Answer my questions or lose your little agency. It will take two phone calls, at most. Is that what you want?"

She sat across from him, as impossibly perfect as ever. Impenetrable, unknowable. It was difficult for him to imagine, now, how desperate he had been to hurl himself against those walls she put up around her and find his way inside.

Just as it was difficult to accept that he had failed.

"I'm not saying that I know what you're talking about," she said after a moment. "But it would seem to me that if a man was such a coward that he required a *service* to end a relationship, that any woman he chose to do that to was better off for it."

"That's a remarkable take, and interestingly enough, absolves you of any culpability." He smiled. "How curious."

"I wouldn't know," she replied, carefully. "But I have to think that if such a service existed, it would profit off the men involved while providing a kind of rescue to the women. Because what decent, honorable man would do such a thing in the first place?"

"Do you think that this argument will work?" He found himself leaning forward, thinking of fragile, sweet Nicolosa's inability to get out of bed. Of that look on her face, as if she'd been kicked. Repeatedly. It was unbearable. "Do you suppose that if you were to go out there and locate all the women you did this to that they would applaud you?"

"Do you think that they wouldn't, in the fullness of time, understand that they dodged a bullet?" she shot back. Then smiled. "Not that I know anything about it, but even hearing about such a service, I have to ask—is wine thrown in their faces? Who is shouted at—the presumably cheating man or the woman he's with?"

And Zago had done his research. He had been on a mission to root out the perpetrators and bring them to some kind of justice since the night his sister had called him in hysterics. And once he'd found the identity of the woman who had come into the apartment that night—and had sat with that a minute—he had gone and found his way to other examples of her work.

For research purposes, naturally.

And it was true. All the drama was focused on the man. The woman he was with usually ran off, often in tears. But if anything was thrown or broken, it was either at the man or belonged to the man.

He hadn't noticed that. It seemed interesting, now, that he hadn't. But he told himself it didn't matter. It couldn't.

"You cannot possibly justify your actions," he told Irinka. "Even if you don't do what you do to the woman. Is a murder any better if it is painless?"

Her smile sharpened. "Comparing a breakup to murder seems a little over the top, doesn't it?"

He didn't think of his sister then. He didn't think of the way Nicolosa had wailed and told him that there was no possible way that Felipe was seeing anyone else.

I might be a fool, his sister had sobbed. *But I'm not that much of a fool. It's entirely possible that he was seeing other women, but if he was, it would have to have been a night here, a night there. There simply wasn't time for him to have the kind of in-depth relationship that woman was screaming about. You have to believe me, Zago. You* have *to.*

And he had believed her. But that wasn't what he thought about now.

It was *this* woman, of all people, telling *him* how a breakup ought to feel.

"I was not at all surprised that the woman who would do these things was you, Irinka," he said after a moment. "Because, as we both know, you have no qualm whatsoever reaching into the chest of another, ripping his heart out, and tossing it to the carrion crows."

He did nothing to prevent the bitterness from coming out in his voice. He did nothing to bank the fury that he could feel cover his face and no doubt take over his gaze.

For the first time in three years, he didn't pretend that the way she'd left was okay.

But this time, it wasn't his own face staring back at him from a mirror while he *didn't* think these things. She was right here.

And she was staring right back at him.

"Is that why you really brought me here?" Irinka asked softly. "All these years later, you want to sit here and conduct a postmortem on our breakup?" She laughed, almost ruefully. "I'll make it simple for you. I was very young. We had nothing in common. I'm no longer quite so young, but the second part still holds. Will I get the private jet back to London or will you be petty and have me find my own way?"

"You're not leaving," he gritted out. But when her brow rose, all cool challenge, he remembered that he was not a caveman. "What I meant to say is, you can leave at will. But I've already outlined the consequences. I would make very certain that you are ready for that. Because in case you've forgotten, I am not a man given to levity. This is not a joke."

"You don't say. And here I've been giggling to myself the whole time, from being swiped off the Portobello Road to being frog marched into this palazzo. The hilarity never ends with you, Zago."

"I don't recall you complaining about my intensity when it mattered." He was moving before he meant to, but then she was, too.

And suddenly they were both standing there in the space between her chair and his settee, the Venetian light filtering in through the ancient windows, pale gold streaming everywhere.

But if there was any oxygen between them, he couldn't find it.

"I haven't complained about anything," she told him, her eyes blazing. "Then or now. I seem to recall that was you."

He laughed, and he hadn't known until that moment that he had sounds like that inside of him. Just as he wasn't sure he knew the man who reached over and slid his hand to take her jaw in his palm.

He didn't grip too hard. He didn't move her about. Zago simply held her there and then, almost fitfully, dragged his thumb over that wicked, tempting, dangerous mouth of hers.

"There you were," he all but crooned. "Parading around as the daughter of one of the most scandalous women alive and vamping it up in her shadow. And only you and I know the truth, don't we?" He leaned in, only a little. He lowered his voice. "It was all an act. Little games you played to keep people at a distance when the truth was, you were an untouched virgin. You played your games then. Now you play them on a dangerous stage. But at the end of the day, we both know that I'm the one who brought you alive. Who put my mouth on every inch of your body, and taught you who you are."

Zago had never said things like that out loud before. But that didn't make them any less true.

Her gaze glittered. "Your arrogance is breathtaking."

"It always was," he agreed. "And even now that I've kidnapped you, brought you to Venice, and have showed myself arrogant once more, what do you think I would find if I slid my hand between your legs, Irinka?"

He shifted closer, until his mouth was nearly on hers. He could see the way her eyes dilated. He could see her pulse go wild in her neck. He could feel the heat of her skin, and later, perhaps, he would explore precisely how it felt to know that everything was as it had always been between them.

Because he was hard, ready, and aching for her as if he had only just had her.

As if there had been no time in between but a few scant minutes instead of years.

"Because between you and me," Zago whispered, "I think we both know that you're already wet. And ready. And hungry. For me, as always."

Something that wasn't as simple as temper, or as complicated as grief, flashed across her face. She lifted a hand to grip his wrist as if she wanted to tear his hand away, but she didn't.

Instead, she leaned closer. "If you wanted to ask me for a date, Zago, you could have texted. Like a normal person."

"Speaking of arrogance," he replied. He let go of her then, though he didn't step back. But then, she didn't, either. "This isn't about you, Irinka, as hard as that might be for you to believe."

"It is difficult, yes," she agreed. "Given the kidnap. And the fact that I'm currently being held in your palazzo, subject to attempts at intimidation. You can see how a person might jump to the conclusion that it was about them."

He ignored that. "This is about my sister. Do you remember her? She was only sixteen back then. And though she is nineteen now, and headed off to university as she should, she is sheltered. Naive." He shook his head. "Knowing this, I made it clear to her that she was to be careful around men, but all that did was keep her from telling me about him when she met him. She knew I wouldn't approve. It was only when he made so many declarations that she felt emboldened." Zago blew out a frustrated breath. "I found what she did tell me sufficiently alarming that I was already planning to go to London, but then instead, you turned up. She was spending the night in his apartment—not for the first time, I am to understand, little as I wish to know these details about my baby sister—and in came this woman making wild accusations and hurling crockery. Nicolosa, bless her, assumed that she and her lover would present a united front, laugh off these accusations, and call the police. But that's not what happened."

He didn't know what he expected her to do. All she did do was gaze back at him with a certain steadiness that suggested to him that she was taking this hard, though he had no evidence to support that. Just a feeling.

And too well did he know how little his feelings ever had to do with reality when it came to Irinka.

"Do you feel good about what you do when you actually know the woman you are paid to destroy?" he asked her. "Because since then, Nicolosa has dropped out of university. She has taken to her bed and refuses to leave her flat in London. She hardly sleeps or eats and if she is awake, she is likely crying."

And he could not bear it, though he did not say that out loud. Zago might have been a ghost in this house, but he had made certain that Nicolosa had a different sort of childhood. He had taken his role as her older brother seriously. Very seriously.

He had cared for her and played with her. As she grew, he had become her mentor, her protector. When there was nothing in these halls but the echoing silence of their father's interest in everything but them, he had told her stories about the people in all the paintings to redirect her attention.

That a man like de Osma had come along and crushed her like this had come terribly close to crushing Zago, too.

Though he did not intend to admit such a thing.

Not to the woman who had been involved in his sister's heartbreak.

"I really am sorry for that," Irinka said quietly, after a moment or two. "I'm sorry that she is so upset. But I cannot be sorry to hear that she was liberated herself from the clutches of a man who has a vibrant reputation for preying upon girls just like her."

"And you are still convinced you are somehow the hero of this tale, are you not? Amazing."

"I notice you're not storming Felipe's residence to demand that he offer you reparation for your sister's broken heart," she retorted. "I'm not surprised that one outrageously wealthy man should find another outrageously wealthy man miraculously without responsibility for his own actions. It must, of course, be my fault."

He didn't point out that she'd essentially admitted it was her, at last. Not that he had been in any doubt.

"Once I knew it was you, I understood," he told her. "For only you, Irinka, are capable of such cruelty. It made all the sense in the world to me that you've made this your profession. After all, I was your first project."

"Is this what you kidnapped me to tell me?" she asked softly, though there was something almost wary in her gaze. "Once again, this really could have been a text." She actually dared roll her eyes at him then, as if this was little more than *an annoyance* to her. As if that's all he was, too. "And while we're on the subject of kidnaps, I told my friends that if they don't hear from me by teatime that they were to involve the authorities. So I hope you're planning on wrapping this up soon."

"I think you'd better call your friends," he said with quiet certainty. "And tell them that you're not coming home. Because we're going to experiment with a little accountability, you and I."

He could see the goose bumps rise along her neck, though she otherwise didn't react. "Are we now?" She dared to look at her watch, another version of a rolled eye. He knew perfectly well it was deliberate. "And how long do you think that will take?"

But when Zago laughed again, it felt more natural this time. "Oh, Irinka. Until we're finally done."

CHAPTER THREE

ALL HE HAD done was put his hand on her face.

It was nothing. *Nothing.*

She kept telling herself that, in the hope that might help her dial it back a bit. That it might counter the outsize reaction she was having to all of this. When it was nothing but a random touch on her chin. Basically like seeing a dentist.

But there'd been his thumb.

And the way he'd moved it across her lips, ragged and searing, igniting old memories she never normally let out in the light of day.

Irinka knew she couldn't let him see her react like this. He was right about one thing—she really had been playing games her whole life. He seemed to think she did that out of some Machiavellian need to manipulate people, which only went to show how little he knew her.

That's a good thing, she chided herself when thinking that made her ache.

She had let him know her well once and look how

that had turned out. He had taught her to avoid that kind of intimacy like the plague. Because it hurt.

And in the end, familiarity really did breed contempt. She had watched that play out in real time between her mother and father. She knew better than to make that same mistake—only here, with Zago, had she ever tried to do the opposite and look how *that* had turned out.

But she did not intend to defend herself to him. He could make all the remarks he wanted about her character, and it wouldn't make any difference.

She knew what had happened here, between them that summer. She knew that *he* had not been one who'd been left broken. Or not the only one. And she also knew that she'd been right to leave while she could, before there was nothing left between them but contempt.

Something she might have told him under different circumstances, secure in the safety of all these years' distance.

Now she would say nothing. Holding his gaze, she made a small spectacle of bending over, reaching into her boot, and pulling out her phone. One of his dark brows rose, suggesting to her that Ms. Thug would be getting a talking-to.

She couldn't really say she minded that.

Irinka glared at him as she straightened. "Some privacy please?"

"There will be very little of that," he assured her.

She sighed and rolled her eyes again, because she'd

seen him react the last time she'd done it. Then she simply opened up the group chat.

Her friends were not entertained by her absence. There were mounting cries for various dramatic responses from some quarters and rather more measured approaches from others, as always.

It's fine, she texted. I'm fine.

And she didn't wait for them to respond, which she knew they would, and likely rapidly. I'm in Venice. It's lovely this time of year.

Is this a cry for help? Maude asked.

Maybe it's code, Lynna added. It doesn't surprise me that Irinka would have various codes, but she never shared any of them with me.

Blink twice if this is really you, Irinka, Auggie added.

Really, I'm fine, Irinka texted back. There's a small matter that needs some attention, that's all. I'll cancel my appointments.

The mobile was snatched out of her hand. She glared up at Zago, outraged. "I beg your pardon."

He scrolled through the chat and slid a dark look her way. "How did three days become teatime?"

"Because it's felt like three years, actually. Give me my mobile back, please?"

He did not. *"Work wives?"* he asked, that cultured voice of his dripping with disdain.

It should not have dripped through her in turn, slow and sweet, like honey.

"That is what my friends and I call ourselves, yes,"

she told him, not quite matching his level of disdain, but she let her smile pick up the slack. "Do you have friends, Zago? If you did, you might also have funny nicknames that you use, shared histories, your own private language made up of anecdotes and memories. Alas."

"I'm fascinated that this is your approach." He apparently satisfied himself with her mobile and handed it back to her, looking as if she'd fallen short in some way. She assured herself that she didn't need him to validate her. It didn't matter what he thought about her friends, her group chat with said friends, or indeed any of her life choices.

What did matter was the fact that when she told herself that, it felt a bit hollow.

But she was in no mood to think about why that might be. "And by 'my approach' do you mean the part where I'm not wailing and lamenting at your feet, begging you to forgive me?" She laughed at that. "The thing is, Zago, I'm not ashamed of what I do. I prefer that you not broadcast it to the world only because that would make it very difficult to keep what I do under the radar, and it might also negatively affect my friends."

Predictably, he looked unmoved.

"If you think that you can lock me away in your little palace—" she began, maybe a little less calmly than she might have liked.

"It is not little, Irinka. I think you know that."

She stared at him. Because it almost sounded as if he meant—

But she refused to go there. "You could keep me locked up here for the rest of my life," she said, saying each word very deliberately. "It still won't make me believe that I'm not providing a necessary service. You might not like it. It might be something more like a mercy killing, if I'm being completely transparent. But every single one of those women who were encouraged to leave the men in question is one less daughter like me, who has had to sit in the presence of His Grace, the perpetually outraged Duke, and listen to him blame me for his inability to wear a condom."

"Seriously hurting innocent people is some kind of crusade, is that it?"

Irinka threw up her hands in the universal sign of exasperation and used that as an opportunity to retreat. She moved away from him, but didn't sit down again. That felt too risky. Instead, she moved almost restlessly toward that balcony, and went outside.

The afternoon was wearing on and the light was like magic, dancing and moving. The trouble with Venice was that it echoed back too well. The past. Her own longings. The things she'd said to him once that she wanted so desperately to deny, but couldn't.

She felt him come up behind her. "Irinka," he began.

But Zago was the most dangerous echo of all.

"Let's discuss the terms of confinement." She turned to face him, leaning back against the rail and

crossing her arms. And she could remember too well
the last time she'd stood here like this, gazing at him.
The tragedy for her was that he had not gotten stooped
and gnarled in the meantime. He was just as tall as she
remembered him. Towering over her when she was
five foot ten in her stocking feet. "Is there a dungeon?
Will there be beatings? What is it going to look like?"

"It's the bravado," he murmured, almost as if he
was whispering some kind of sweet nothing. "It just
astonishes me. Is there nothing I can say to you to
make you accept the gravity of the situation?"

Irinka tilted her head to one side as she gazed at
him. "Is that really what you want, Zago? Me writh-
ing about in abject terror that I might have put myself on the wrong side of your good opinion? Is that
the kind of thing that excites you when you wake up
from a dream in the middle of the night?"

"Even now, you attempt to provoke me." And there
was something about the way he said it. It was calm,
yes. That was alarming enough. Yet there was almost
something like satisfaction in his voice. Like he had
expected this. "But you forget that I know you."

She sighed at that. "You barely knew a girl that I
haven't been for years."

What she did not say was that the girl he'd brought
to this palazzo was not the girl who had left it only a
few months later. He would probably love to hear that
he had *made her a woman*, but not in the way people
usually meant it when they said such things. It wasn't
simply because he had taken her virginity. Or, more

accurately, because she'd given him her virginity in an explosion of joy and heat and desire.

It was that walking away from him had changed her almost as profoundly as what happened between them had.

Irinka had never been the same.

And she had not had the option to cry for a month, not that she begrudged his sister her wallow. But Irinka hadn't had a benevolent father figure to look after her. She'd had to figure out a life for herself, one way or another.

And unless she wanted to tell her friends what had happened, she'd had to pretend that nothing had.

She'd gone for door number two. And only occasionally felt guilty about it.

But her experience here had made it clear to her that no one could handle *all* of her, not even her friends. They benefited as much as anyone else from the way Irinka flitted in and out, never quite pinned down, allowing them to enjoy her without ever having to deal with the *too much* part.

She had learned that here.

There was no possible way that Zago could know the woman she'd become *because* of him.

"My sister has been wretched for an entire month," he told her now, that gleaming menace in his gaze that, sadly, only made him that much hotter. It was desperately unfair. "Thirty-some days is a long time. Why don't you and I start with a month."

It wasn't really a question. Much less an invitation.

"A month of what?" she asked, as if it really was some kind of invitation and she was mulling it over. "Why don't you lay out the parameters? Depending on what you say, I'll decide if I need to attempt to jump off this balcony right now."

Maybe Zago really did know her, because he took a moment to look over the side and then back at her, one dark eyebrow raised. "I wouldn't recommend it. It's steeper than it looks and it won't be a soft landing."

Irinka let her chin jut upward. "Don't threaten me with a good time." And then she made herself smile. "I mean it. Thirty days of what?"

"You can pick your labor." He said this as if he was granting her a great favor. "I've always fancied a personal housemaid. Perhaps you can cook and clean and wow me with your domestic prowess." That brow stayed lifted. "Or you could work it out in trade."

He said that lightly enough, but she couldn't be certain that he was kidding. Not with that look on his face, that dark promise that she knew he was fully capable of answering.

Too well did she know it.

She blew out a breath through pursed lips, then shook her head. "That does sound like labor. House-maiding, that is."

"Irinka. Please. What do you know about cooking or cleaning?"

"I love that you really imagine that you're some-how the better choice. It must be truly spectacular to be a man." She waved her hand at him, taking in his whole...dark gold magnificence. She made herself look something like scornful. Taken aback. "I can get that anywhere, Zago. It gets thrown at me on the street, left and right. What do you think would compel me to sleep with a man who thinks as little of me as you do? What could be the possible benefit?"

"Very well, then," he said, not rising to debate the way she wanted him to do. "A new addition to the household staff. I will notify the *maggiordomo*."

What bothered Irinka was that he could be talking about *servitude* and she could still want him to so much. She had to question what exactly she was doing, and why it irked her that he was so *calm*. Did she want him to crack? Did she want him to boil over so that anything that happened after could be blamed on him? His temper, his overreach, his problem?

She was afraid she already knew the answer and it didn't exactly cover her in glory.

In that moment, she decided she *would* stay. It was all fun and games up to now—in the sense of not being fun at all and hating that she needed to play games in the first place—but she got the distinct impression that he expected her to...have a meltdown, perhaps? Rage at him that she could obviously not be expected to do either thing?

Irinka wondered what third option he had up his sleeve, and she refused to give him the opportunity to think that he was right about her. Or knew her.

At all.

Besides, as her mother always said, *Without hard work there is no getting fish from the pond.*

Meaning that the pain of the hard work got the necessary results.

Irinka could scrub a few floors if that would do the trick. Because proving Zago wrong would be its own reward. And if he exploded in the middle of it? Had a full-on temper tantrum and lost all access to this *calmness* of his? Even better.

Her mother wasn't the only one who only liked fishing when real fish weren't involved.

"I'm glad we worked that out," she said sweetly. "I can't wait to see what servants' quarters look like in a whole palazzo."

The last time she'd stayed here it had been in his vast, glorious bedroom that had made it clear that if this was a palace, he was its king. Today, he only laughed that dark, affecting laugh once more and then turned on his heel, beckoning her to follow him through the palazzo, but this time away from where she knew that bedroom was.

Irinka told herself she was *glad.*

He climbed the grand stair, then moved toward the back of the grand house, taking her all the way up to the very top where the roof was slanted and the rooms were tiny. The actual servants' quarters, just as she'd requested.

She supposed that he expected her to start weeping and wailing, begging to be taken down to some fancy part of the palazzo that better suited the daughter of a duke.

The joke was on him. She had been raised by Roksana, who liked to tell dark and disturbing stories about her childhood while simultaneously complaining that everyone in her adopted country was so *soft*. Squishy, even. Roksana was not a fan of coddling or anything else that might make life easy. She had been at great pains to make certain that her daughter was hardier than most.

Especially once her father had acknowledged her existence. And his paternity.

These are not gifts that he gives you, she would say. *These are your birthright. But they will also make you a soft target if you are not careful.*

The upshot of that was that Irinka had often slept on a pallet on the floor in their flat, her bed being deemed off-limits to her whenever her mother felt she was losing her edge.

The little room that Zago showed her into was a major upgrade from a pallet. It had a solid bed, a small chest of drawers, and a hanging rack for any clothes Irinka might have had with her if she hadn't been swiped up off the Portobello Road on a Tuesday morning.

"How homey," Irinka said brightly. She turned to him and beamed. "When do I report for duty?"

"I believe the kitchen feeds the staff in an hour," he replied stiffly. "I will inform the *maggiordomo* that you are to be put straight to work."

Again he paused, as if expecting pushback.

"Can't wait," she replied, smiling widely.

And then Irinka had the pleasure of seeing what she was pretty sure was temper on his face before he left her there, closing the door decisively behind him.

"Worth it," she murmured into the quiet of the little room.

She stood there a moment, listening to his footsteps retreat. Then she went and sat on the bed, wondering if that heartbeat of hers would ever slow down again. She put her hand on her chest and held it there, as if that could soothe her treacherous heart into behaving.

As if anything was going to be a balm on the wound that was Zago, when nothing ever had been.

Irinka felt that same buried sob in her chest. She felt a telltale kind of itch at the back of her eyes. But she stayed where she was, breathing steadily, until it went away.

Only then did she go to the window on the back side of the palazzo and look out. It wasn't the Grand Canal there before her. It was red-tiled roofs and church spires, domes and makeshift viewing platforms, narrow canals with gondolas aplenty and wooden walkways that ran alongside them.

She heard bells in the distance. The light changed constantly, dancing into the shadows of the old city, and seemed to come from a different sun that shone down elsewhere.

Maybe it was because everything here was doomed. Venice was sinking, everyone knew that.

Maybe it was as magical as it was because it had never been meant to last.

Though thinking such things made the urge to sob come back, and she didn't want that.

Irinka pulled out her mobile again, canceled all of her pending appointments, and then opened her messages to find her three friends in a flurry of speculation.

Maybe I'm wrong, Auggie had texted, but didn't Irinka go to Venice the summer after we graduated from uni?

I think you know that she did, Lynna replied. And when she came back, she was oddly brittle.

Irinka took exception to that. Oddly brittle? She had been nothing of the sort. She had been marching around in the new life they were building together like a proper soldier with a broken heart, and none of them had been any the wiser.

She had *protected* them from her pain.

I gave her flowers of hope and plants of remembrance, Maude chimed in.

The funny thing was that Irinka remembered those flowers. They had been bright, happy peonies that she would never have bought for herself, too afraid of being *soft*. And the plants—bright, bold, green things she wouldn't have the slightest idea how to identify— were still in the office, still going strong, in complete defiance of Irinka's noted black thumb.

Do we suppose the sudden, pressing matter is in fact a boy? Auggie asked.

Irinka would be the absolute last person to share her private life even with her closest friends, Lynna replied. So I couldn't possibly speculate. By which I mean yes, clearly a boy.

Rose, hawthorn, and lemon balm for heartbreak, Maude added. It makes a lovely tea.

Irinka couldn't take it. Venice is actually one of the foremost holiday destinations on the planet, she found herself typing. Furiously. A person doesn't need a reason to go to Venice. Venice exists. That's reason enough.

Now she's a travelogue, Auggie observed.

Lynna sent a thumbs-up emoji. And then: This sudden love for Venice is more than I knew about Irinka five minutes ago, anyway.

It turns out that the brother of one of the women that Felipe was toying with took exception to the way his sister's relationship ended, Irinka wrote, hoping her frosty tone was making it into the text bubbles. We're discussing the moral ramifications.

…That sounds dangerous, Maude wrote.

It is not dangerous at all, Irinka assured them. It is actually very boring. I'm perfectly capable of handling men, as you might recall, given it is in fact MY JOB.

Is he hot? Auggie asked. Irinka decided that was enough texting for the day.

Also, it was a ridiculous question. Was Zago hot? Was the earth round? Was Venice the most achingly beautiful place she'd ever seen?

None of that was worth answering, because there was only one answer.

She decided to leave her room and take a wander down the hall, where she found a sitting room that looked softly lived in, and a lavatory that was clearly communal. That was fair enough. It reminded her of living in halls at university. Irinka splashed water on her face and wished that she had a toothbrush.

Then she wandered downstairs, even though she knew it wasn't quite time to present herself in the kitchens yet.

When she made it down to the bottom of the great stair, she stopped and looked toward the great door. She knew that if she raced through it, she'd be out in that courtyard. And if she wanted, she could flag someone down on the Grand Canal, maybe steal a boat if there was one at the dock, even take her chances with a swim—

But instead of doing any of that, she simply stood there.

It was almost as if she didn't want to leave.

And she didn't understand. Surely she should be itching at the chance. She should have heaved herself through the door and taken her chances.

But there was nothing in her that wanted to do that. It was like her body was protesting the very notion on a deep, bone level.

Irinka turned back toward the palazzo, away from her bid for freedom, and then went still.

Because Zago stood there at the top of the flight of grand, imposing stairs, watching her.

"Did you think I was going to run away?" she asked.

Though she sounded a good deal *throatier* than she'd intended.

"I'm wondering why you haven't," he replied.

She was too, despite her desire to go fishing earlier. But the moment he said that, she stopped caring about it and made herself shrug with as much nonchalance as she could manage.

"I've always wanted the opportunity to play Cinderella," she told him as if this really was nothing but a jolly lark. "I'm rather disappointed that there aren't cinders and ash in my little garret room." She held her arms away from her, indicating the clothes she'd put on for a rainy London morning. It seemed like a lifetime ago now. "I do hope you have some rags for me. That will really set the scene."

He shook his head, almost sadly, as he came down those wide steps and was once again standing in front of her. And she couldn't deny the heat between them, as wild as ever. Or that she recognized instantly that the scent that seemed to wind all around her was something she often thought she smelled in her dreams. Something like spice but unidentifiable.

She had never smelled anything like it.

When she dropped her hands back to her sides, she hit herself in the thighs a little harder than necessary, like that might snap her out of this.

"Still playing your games," he said, almost sorrowfully, but that heat in his gaze was more like temper. "I wonder what will happen when the gameplaying ends. And it is only you and me, the truth of things, lying unvarnished between us."

"For that to happen, you would have to also stop playing games. And I don't think you're in any mood to do that, are you?" He looked as if he might respond, but she shook her head. "Don't kid yourself, Zago. I wasn't the only person in that relationship that summer. I was just the one who left before we burned ourselves alive."

Then she stepped around him, carefully, because the urge to simply melt into him was so strong that she was afraid that she might accidentally succumb to it. And then find herself in his arms without meaning to, and then what would she do?

Because one thing she knew entirely too well was that untangling herself from this man's touch, from the way he looked at her, not to mention how he made her *feel*, seemed impossible. Clearly she hadn't done a great job after the last time.

So she made her way around him almost gingerly— keeping her distance—and then headed off toward the kitchen to start playing her assigned role to perfection.

Because she was pretty sure that if she did, she might drive him mad.

A goal worth aiming for, she thought. So Irinka was smiling as she went.

CHAPTER FOUR

IT HAD NOT occurred to Zago that she would choose menial labor.

He thought that merely suggesting that she take to his bed to save her little business would lead to cracks in that armor of hers—because they both knew that whatever else that had happened between them, what had happened in his bed had been honest.

Scorchingly so.

Zago had certainly never intended to pressure her into his bed, not least because he did not think that *pressure* would be required. But he was also not averse to using whatever tools he could to come to a place that felt like justice when it came to her. And him. And Nicolosa most of all.

If he'd really thought she would sleep with him on demand, as some kind of payment, he would never have offered it as an option. Because in all his fantasies about what it might be like to have another night with Irinka—not that he admitted that such notions haunted him—in not a single one of them was the heat between them *transactional*.

He'd assumed that she would not wish to get intimate with him, because there had been too much honesty there and that had clearly been too much for her. He had intended to greatly enjoy watching her try to play one of her little roles with him, here.

There was no way she could do it. He was sure of it, and he'd intended to take great pleasure in watching her try.

Zago had rather thought that claiming she needed to spend a month in his bed was a bit of a taste of her own medicine. Strange things happened when a person messed around with other people's emotions. He had wanted to give her a much-needed object lesson.

Before she'd appeared at the palazzo, he may also have imagined that her power over him would be lessened, but still. He knew that in the end he was a man of honor.

He had never been anything else.

All Zago had wanted was to make her think twice about this role she played—the role that had led directly to his beloved sister's unhappiness.

He had thrown out the option for domestic service as more of a nuclear option, so perhaps he shouldn't have been surprised that the impossible woman chose it.

Then again, revenge could take many forms. Apparently she chose the menial route.

At first, he didn't think that she would really go through with it.

"Your expectation is that I put an Englishwoman

of noble blood to work in the kitchens?" his *maggiordomo*, the austere Roderigo, asked in astonishment when Zago informed him of the addition to his staff. "Surely not. Surely I am misunderstanding your intent."

"That is exactly my intent," Zago told this man who had looked at him in the same exacting manner when Zago had been an unsupervised child and given to sliding down the banisters of ancient stairs in this place. "I think that daily chores will be just the thing *because* she is an Englishwoman of noble blood. Though half of her is quite Russian, if you are concerned."

He did not think it germane to mention that Roksana, who was still emblazoned on the covers of magazines with regularity, was no one's stereotype of any hardy Russian peasant, grimly tilling a field.

"With respect," Roderigo ventured. And he paused, as if considering the parameters of that respect. Or perhaps if he wished to show any respect at all in the face of such extraordinary events… But the man's lifetime of service to the Baldissera family clearly won the day. By a razor-thin margin. "It is only that I'm not certain you understand the care that goes into maintaining the palazzo. For anyone to be accepted to work here requires a great deal of training, no matter how menial the labor."

"I trust you," Zago said, his patience about as thin as that margin. And Roderigo immediately inclined his head, because he had not lowered himself to arguing with a member of the family in the span of any-one's memory. No matter the provocation.

He expected Roderigo to come back almost at once, Irinka in tow, because he could not imagine her working—*really working*—any more than Roderigo could.

Yet that night went by and there was no sign of her. The next morning, he woke early, expecting half the staff to be lined up outside his door with lists of their complaints about her princess behavior and in-ability to complete the tasks *they* did by rote, but the hallway was empty when he looked.

He was forced to demean himself and start skulk-ing around until he could find her himself.

And when he did, he stopped in astonishment.

Because when she'd stayed here before, he didn't think she'd ever risen before noon. Partly because they had stayed up half the night, so perhaps that wasn't a fair assessment of how she normally greeted a new day. But still, it was barely six in the morning today. Early by any measure.

And the infamous socialite daughter of scandal and notoriety that was Irinka Scott-Day was not re-clining in an eye mask somewhere. She was out with the rest of the maids, scrubbing the steps that led up into the palazzo. The way they did every morning, and much of the courtyard as well, to get the salt off from the canals' brackish water.

She didn't even look like herself. Someone had given her clothes and they were too baggy, and certainly not of the quality she generally preferred. Her hair was in two braids tight to her head in front and then woven together at the back. It was the sort of hairstyle that he thought would be better served under a tiara. In some ballroom somewhere.

Not scrubbing the steps.

Zago didn't like it. Though he could not have said why.

And he certainly shouldn't have found it appealing, despite his best efforts to quell it, that she seemed to take so easily to something that should have broken her. That had been engineered to break her, in fact.

But she was anything but broken. Irinka seemed to have no trouble whatsoever pitching in with the rest of them, as if she'd spent every day of her life doing absolutely nothing but scrubbing floors. When he knew that wasn't the case. Everyone knew it wasn't. Her manicure alone announced the truth of things without her having to say a word.

And yet even more strangely, the other maids seemed to have no trouble with her. There were no rolling eyes behind her back, no whispers, no quickly hidden smiles of disdain.

This was not at all how he'd planned this.

But if she could be so stubborn, then so too could he.

A few more days passed, and Zago continued to receive no bad reports about Irinka's tenure as a new staff member. He received no reports about Irinka at all, for that matter.

It had been a week when he finally caved and asked Roderigo.

"I keep expecting to hear complaints about your newest hire," he said that evening, watching the sun set on the canal, a pageant of bright colors mixed into the water until it was all the same gleaming mystery.

It made him think of Irinka even more and he resented it.

"It is the most extraordinary thing," said Roderigo, sounding almost…overawed?

Zago looked at him, a bit narrowly. This from a man who had distinguished himself by failing to be impressed by anything, always. He had been running this house since before Zago was born and in all that time he had always remained resolutely under-awed by every person of means and consequence he'd encountered.

It was part of why Zago trusted him so implicitly.

"Don't tell me that you have fallen under her spell," Zago murmured. He swirled his *aperitivo* in its heavy crystal tumbler. "I am astounded at you, Roderigo."

The older man seemed as unimpressed with *him* as ever. He regarded Zago, his employer, with a cool eye. "Everyone knows precisely who she is, of course. Most of us remember when she was here before. And yet never could we have imagined that when put to the test, she would rise to meet it so beautifully."

"Beautifully," Zago repeated in disbelief.

"I suppose we are all of us given to our biases," the older man said then, in a philosophical tone of voice that Zago had never heard come from dour Roderigo in all his life. "I would expect a fine young lady such as the *signorina* to not only be emotionally unprepared to work as we do, but to be physically incapable as well. And yet she has been unflagging and enthusiastic in turn. She is the first one up in the morning and the last still working at night." He sighed, and appeared to remember himself, taking on his habitual *almost* frown. "I only wish this were not some bargain between the two of you, for I would hire her on the spot."

That was precisely what Zago did not wish to hear. He eyed the man who had in many ways raised him somewhat balefully. "I'm delighted to hear it."

The old man stopped pretending that he was polishing the statuary and fixed his employer with a narrow glare. "At the risk of overstepping—"

"Is that considered a risk in this house? I thought it was considered a perk of employment."

Roderigo ignored him. "There is a point at which a person can become blinded to the reality of things, too busy are they focusing on the past. Making it the present, when it cannot be. It can *never* be. And then it, too, is lost to time."

If his *maggiordomo* had hauled off and gut punched him, he would not have been any more surprised.

"Thank you," Zago replied after a moment, and even that was a challenge. "That will be all."

Roderigo inclined his head and withdrew so gracefully that it only made Zago feel churlish.

He had not bargained for this.

To be haunted by her even more than usual, because he knew that she was sleeping under this roof.

To think that at any moment he might turn a corner in his own home and find her there, shooting him an insolent look from those too-blue eyes and then carry on with some menial task as if he did not exist.

He had created the situation, he understood that. But it was still insupportable. It was *agony*.

And perhaps that was how he found himself moving through the house much later that night, telling himself that he did not wish to disturb anyone and that was why he remained so quiet.

Or perhaps that was simply a matter of plausible deniability.

If anyone had seen him, or heard him, then it was possible he might have thought better of what he was doing.

But no one did.

And Zago kept going, as if drawn through the house by a force outside his control.

He climbed the stairs in dim light until he found his way to the servants' quarters, and it was as if he was in a dream when he was, at last, standing at her door.

Drawn to her as he was when he slept, because he had certainly had a version of this dream before now. Many, many versions of it. More than he cared to admit. All of them with him standing outside a room, a house, and knowing she was within.

All of that longing and grief, despair and desire.

But he was awake this time, alive with this wanting—this need—that tore him inside out whether he indulged it or did not.

And he was aware that there were too many truths *just there*, simmering beneath the surface—

But Zago was not in the mood to sift through such detritus, so he put his hand to the door, opened it up, and stepped inside.

And Irinka, damn her, merely gazed back at him as if she had been expecting him all along.

As if his sudden appearance did not faze her in the least.

She was sitting on her bed, wearing something sloppy and oversize that both hid her figure and accentuated it. She set aside the book she was reading with every appearance of complete serenity and only the faintest hint of irritation, as if she had been having a pleasant evening and was preparing herself—bracing herself—for the excessively minor annoyance that was Zago.

And something in him, something doused in the fuel of that summer three years ago and the reckoning that so far wasn't...*ignited*.

That he should be haunted, pursued by her ghost through his own home, while she sat here so calmly. Reading a book. Completely at her ease and unbothered by all of this.

"I hope you are enjoying yourself," he managed to say, though his voice felt thick on his own tongue.

"I am," she replied with more of that perfect equanimity that made his skin feel six sizes too small. "I feel as if I'm on a spiritual retreat, Zago. Isn't that how a person transcends their ordinary little life? A bit of labor, a bit of chanting, a monastic cell, and ample time to interrogate one's thoughts? I'm certain I will achieve enlightenment at any moment."

It was that arch, amused voice of hers, and he hated it. That cocktail party version of her, brittle and witty in all the worst ways. It was the kind of wit that was too sharp, too unpredictable. The sort that created barriers, when his memories of her were all blurred boundaries, the two of them tangled and entwined in every possible way.

"Why are you looking at me like that?" Her eyebrows rose, and she made no attempt to soften the challenge in her expression. "Is this not what you wanted? A reckoning writ large upon my immortal soul while engaged in a good, old-fashioned mortification of the flesh? It's all so hair-shirted and Catholic. I must be in Italy."

And when he planned this, down to fetching her off the street in England, he had done so with great forethought. He had been careful, plotting it all out like a chess game. If this, then that. If not that, then this. He had allowed for every possible move and had arranged multiple countermoves to address each, or so he'd thought.

But he hadn't planned for *this*.

For her to be almost like a different person altogether.

Colder. Harder.

"You have changed," he told her, darkly.

She regarded him coolly, which was at least some kind of improvement on *mild annoyance*. "You taught me a very important lesson, Zago. And don't think I'm not grateful. Before you, I had no idea that I was so susceptible to the kinds of nonsense that other girls indulge in. You showed me that I was no better than any of them. That there was no need to pretend otherwise. And once I accepted that part of myself, I found the true strength that my mother always tried to bring out in me." She smirked. "Kudos."

Something in him simply snapped.

Zago moved to the bed and he reached for her, hauling her into the air and then setting her on her feet before him.

"I cannot understand the game you're playing," he gritted out. "This is simply a role you're playing, like all the others. Because you know and I know that what happened between us was no silly girl's daydream. You know and I know *exactly* what this was."

"I have no idea what you're talking about," she threw at him, but there was a storm in her gaze.

He leaned closer, his hands curling around her shoulders to draw her closer. Or perhaps it was that he bent closer to her, he couldn't tell.

It hardly mattered.

"I told you not to lie to me," he said, so close that it was almost a kiss. "I warned you."

She made a sound of frustration, or perhaps it was the same need that shouted in him, and then she surged forward and up onto her toes to crash her mouth to his.

And the world shifted all around them once more.

This kaleidoscope, this catastrophe.

Every color in the world shattered and brought together, over and over again, every time her tongue touched his.

She angled her head and his hands moved so he could lift her into the air, because he knew what she would do even as she did it—wrapping her legs around his waist and hooking her arms around his neck.

There is nothing cold about *this* Irinka. There was nothing chilly, no barbed comments, no *serene irritation*.

There was only the impossible firestorm that had raged between them from the start.

He could remember it too well, especially now he had her in his arms once more.

He kissed her and kissed her, holding her up and reveling once again at how perfectly they fit together, how exquisitely their bodies seemed to know each other too well.

And he remembered.

That night at the beginning of that summer, looking up from a questionably modernized version of *La*

Traviata at La Teatro Fenice, only to catch her eye during the interval.

And Zago had never believed in the kind of electric shock that could stop a man in his tracks, change his life, and make him over to someone new at a glance.

He had never believed that it was possible to look at a woman, feel hollowed out within, and never feel whole again unless he was with her.

And yet he had moved with single-minded purpose toward her, the very moment he'd seen her. He couldn't remember who she had been there with, or why. Nothing had existed for him but the girl with the blue eyes and the jet-black hair—and that look of shocked recognition that they had shared.

It all happened so fast.

He had left this very house that night one version of himself and had come back a different man entirely.

And in all these years since that night, since the summer that had followed it, he had questioned that feeling. He had almost convinced himself that it had been some kind of summer fever, not uncommon in Venice. And he had been something like relieved to discover it had shifted into a certain, driving coldness when he'd realized she was involved with Nicolosa's heartbreak.

But now the truth was here, in his arms, and he was changed anew.

Just as it had three years ago, everything escalated.

His hands moved, finding her bare skin beneath the baggy clothes she wore.

She moaned against his mouth and somehow they were moving, tangling up with each other on that tiny bed that barely fit her, much less the two of them.

But there was something about the situation that made it hotter.

Breathless and wild.

Neither one of them spoke. And there was no need to issue warnings, for surely the both of them were equally aware that most of the palazzo's staff slept nearby.

So it was all breath and hands, tongues and teeth. They wrestled and moved, relearning each other in a blistering rush of heat, moving with each other and against each other and into each other, until he found himself lying on his back with his hands wrapped around her hips.

He lifted her, his gaze finding her as the light neither one of them had bothered to turn off bathed them both in its glare.

Zago could see her perfectly—no dream, no blur—as Irinka pushed herself up on her knees, braced herself against the wall of his chest, and then lowered herself down on him—

And not slowly. She did not *ease* her way.

She was soft and wet, he was huge, and she made a whimpering sound as she took him in, hard and fast.

He pulled her down, smoothing his hand down the length of her spine and holding her face to his chest as she panted. That took some time. Then, slowly, she adjusted, moving her hips incrementally as she tried to accommodate him.

As she relearned him and how deep and wide he filled her.

It had taken a long time that first time, three years ago. It had taken him bringing her to pleasure with his mouth, his fingers. Testing her and teasing her until she was mindless and begging him and bargaining.

Only then did he press inside her body, and he'd done it slowly. It had been a sweet, exquisite torment.

But he had not hurt her.

"Why did you do that?" he asked, there at her ear.

"Maybe," she replied, her face still buried in his chest, "you are not the only one who wanted a reckoning."

Irinka pushed herself up then, and stunned him anew. Her hair was a wreck now, made messy by his hands. It flowed all around her and she still wore what he thought must be some discarded man's T-shirt someone in the house had donated to her, because it drooped off the side of her shoulder. But it gave him tantalizing glimpses of her breasts beneath. And he left it on because he could still slide his hands up and fill his palms with her. He could still pull her closer, and play with her nipples through the thin material with his mouth, because it drove her wild.

But she gazed down at him, and there was moisture in the corner of her eyes, and a tear or two on her cheek, wiped hastily away.

And something about her was so fierce that it made him ache.

Only then did she press her palms hard against his abdomen, and begin to move.

And the glory of this, the sheer, mad wonder, leveled him.

Ruined him.

"If I were you," he told her in a dark whisper, "I would hurry."

Then, at last, she was wholly and entirely the girl he'd known that summer. Her lips curved into something wicked and knowing.

And because she was Irinka, she immediately slowed.

Zago let her play. The way she lowered herself, the way she moved her hips. The way she rocked against him, bracing herself as she did it. He let her experiment with all of these things.

He let her set the pace, the rhythm.

But he also trailed a hand up and over her belly, beneath that shirt, and then tugged her down so she could play her games while his tongue was in her mouth, and he could meet that fire with fire of his own.

With his other hand, he reached between them and pressed down hard, just above the place where they were joined.

And Irinka shattered immediately.

She shattered and she screamed, but he swallowed

the sound, taking all of it in his mouth and holding her as she shook and shook.

He kept thrusting into her, harder and harder, as she soared off one peak and then flew higher toward another.

Zago moved back, flipping her over and coming up to hold her close. Then he thrust deep, losing any rhythm save the one they made together, until she was thrown off that cliff once more.

And this time, as she began to calm down, he slowed and spent some time toying with her, too.

Because turnabout was fair play.

"You're a demon," she whispered, half a sigh and half a groan.

"You're welcome," he replied.

But the next time she shattered, he buried his face in her neck, and went with her.

CHAPTER FIVE

IRINKA TOLD HERSELF that one small, inconsequential slip didn't have to *mean* anything.

Zago had stayed in her room that night because neither one of them seemed able to move. They had slept together in that tiny, narrow bed and that had done her no good. She could admit that much. It was too much like all those dreams she'd had, except in a narrow bed like that there was no possibility that every part of her was not touching every part of him.

His scent was the only thing she could smell. He was every breath she took.

She slept and dreamed of him, woke and he was still there, and then it was so easy to simply turn in her sleep and meet him again. And feel him move deep inside of her.

And she had forgotten, that first time, that he really was that big. Long and thick and so hard it made her melt just thinking of it. But that did not mean she needed to slam herself onto him again and again in a kind of desperation that felt like the sharper edge of need.

In any case, he did not seem inclined to allow it.

So even in the dark, half-asleep in the middle of the night, he took his time. He moved his fingers through her slippery heat, making her bite down hard on his shoulder as she burst into flame, then shook all over him.

Only then did he find her molten core and push in, deep.

Only then did he set them both afire until, once again, there was little left of them but ash.

When Irinka woke again, it was morning. The very early morning, and her alarm was going off, and part of her thought that being with Zago was simply a dream. That same dream that she always had.

The dream that had taken her too long to wake up from, even when she'd limped back to England that summer, soft and bruised from the force of all those terrible emotions. Just as her mother had always warned her. She had slept on the floor for months to toughen herself up.

To make sure she would never be *soft* like that again.

But when she sat up, she could feel him all over her body. She was sore in a very specific, deeply satisfying way that made every nerve in her body feel more alive than she had in ages.

Her tiny little room was empty but she was naked in her bed, when Irinka never slept naked. And his shirt was one of the items of clothing strewn about on the floor.

Just in case she intended to keep telling herself she'd dreamed it all.

She went and picked up his shirt, betraying herself entirely when she held it to her face, breathing him in once more.

"Like a bloody addict," she muttered to herself.

Not that thinking that stopped her.

But time was moving along and so she made herself head down the hall to the shower just the same, having learned quickly enough that if she set her alarm just a half hour earlier than everyone else's, she could take her time. Today, she needed it.

And by the time she emerged from all that hot water, she was resolute once more.

There was no denying that she and Zago had chemistry. There was a part of her that was grateful to discover that they still did, that she hadn't been *quite* so foolish a girl as she liked to remember when she thought of that summer. If anything, that chemistry was even stronger now than it had been then.

But *Chemistry is what makes bombs,* Roksana liked to say.

And so Irinka did not go and find him, despite the minor ruckus in her body that urged her to do just that. Instead, she marched herself back down to the kitchen and went back to work.

She worked all day, the way she always did here. And while she had certainly enjoyed needling Zago about the *mortification of her flesh*, such as it was, the truth was that there really was something about this work that she liked.

Irinka was fully aware that part of her ability to enjoy it was because this wasn't actually her life. She was not doomed to scrub floors and steps and clean some rich man's antiques forever. And she knew herself well enough to know that if it had been her life, she would have been far less enamored of it.

But as a break from her life, it was amazing how satisfying it was. She was given concrete tasks and all she had to do was complete them. And when she was finished, she had either achieved what she'd been asked to do or she had not. There was no wiggle room—something was either dusted or dirty. There was no intense problem-solving. No inhabiting roles and gauging every room she walked into so that she could adjust her performance accordingly, and quickly.

No one in this house expected her to be anything but what she was: *il padrone*'s one-time lover back here playing Cinderella games.

It was remarkably freeing.

So much so that it was causing her to think about her life back in London in a way she hadn't in years. To ask herself if what she was doing was sustainable, especially now that all of her friends had found happiness with their new loves in ways that Irinka applauded—for them—but certainly did not understand.

Because the changes her friends had gone through

lately raised an interesting question that she kept finding herself pondering as she scrubbed and dusted and polished. She was the one who had made a great many of the contacts that had kept His Girl Friday solvent all these years. But if all of her friends were set for life now, and could work not to survive, but to please themselves…was it necessary for Irinka to continue *her* work, too?

Did she do it because she liked it? Or because the agency needed it?

Or maybe, something in her whispered, *it has a bit more to do with the horrible wealthy man who treated your mother—and you—like actual rubbish to be tossed aside in the street, and you thought you might as well go in where smarter heads might fear to tread and help cut a bit of that* waste removal *off at the pass?*

She couldn't answer that—or she didn't want to, because what did that say about her and her childhood trauma, how embarrassing that she'd never thought about that before—so while she mulled it all over she let the housework soothe her. On her lunch break she huddled at the back of the palazzo near the narrower canal used for deliveries and frowned out at the water and the steep sides of ancient buildings that rose all around. There were no walkways here, only steep sides and no boats, or she might have felt honor bound to attempt an escape no matter how *soothing* it was to make glass gleam.

Irinka was not foolish enough to tell her friends

any of these things. They would all be on the next plane, rushing to her rescue, because they would assume that she had suffered some kind of head injury if she was extolling the virtues of being a domestic servant.

And she did not need rescuing. She never had.

This is all very mysterious, Auggie pointed out in the text chain later that night. Irinka, have you moved to Venice forever? Since when do you keep secrets from us?

I always keep secrets from you, Irinka replied. This you know.

I thought the entire point of Irinka was that she's endlessly and needlessly secretive, Lynna agreed.

Secrets, Maude chimed in, are like walled gardens.

Irinka stared at that text, baffled. And also flooded with the usual surge of affection she felt for Maude and her gardens.

Yes, she texted back. Exactly that.

And she wasn't particularly surprised when her door opened once again, on the other side of midnight.

"Some people knock and wait to be invited in," she pointed out.

"Some people lock their door," Zago replied.

This time he simply crossed to the bed and climbed into it. And she turned to him without any further words and slowly, carefully, *recklessly* they pulled each other into pieces.

And this went on, one week into the next.

Until one night, as they lay there tangled into their usual knot, panting into the crooks of each other's necks, he shifted so he could look down at her.

"I think I've had enough of this," he said.

"That's a crying shame," Irinka murmured. She moved her hips sinuously and smiled when his eyes went blank, because she could feel him harden inside of her. "I'll miss this."

"That is not at all what I mean," Zago replied in that dark way that thrilled her, because she could feel it in her bones.

He stood then, pulled on the trousers he'd worn here only to toss them off upon arrival, and then picked her up. He did not bother to cover her. And Irinka couldn't decide if she was startled, horrified, or wildly entertained when he simply walked out of her room and carried her through the house.

The palazzo was quiet all around them, but those famous paintings on the walls seemed to look askance at her, no doubt as taken aback as she was.

Zago carried her in no great hurry through the grand palace until he reached his own suite and then installed her in his bed.

Where she hadn't been since that summer, but that didn't bear thinking about just then.

"But *il padrone*," Irinka said, smirking at him, "I am but a servant girl."

"I wish you were," he growled at her. "I wish you were anything that simple."

He then demonstrated his feelings on the topic by

tying her to the bedposts, because there, in his bed-chamber, no one would hear her when she screamed out her pleasure.

So she did.

In the morning she woke to find the light stream-ing in, which meant that it was late. She sat up in a rush, then froze.

Because Zago was there, lounging in the sitting area near the great fireplace. There was no fire at this time of year, and she thought that was a pity, because even during the stifling-hot summer she'd spent here she'd wished for one.

Though she supposed they'd made their own.

He did not look up from the newspaper that he was reading with a skeptical look on his face. "How nice of you to join us this morning."

"You have made me unpardonably late for my du-ties," she said. "The staff will be in an uproar."

"They are far too well trained for that," Zago said. He took his time setting the paper aside. And then gazed at her. "I'm sorry to tell you that your tenure as a housemaid has come to an end, Irinka."

He was so beautiful that he made her throat hurt. She could feel a lump forming there, and an ache in her ribs, because something about this man made her feel blurry all over.

As if, given half a chance, she would throw herself into him and disappear.

Three years ago the prospect had terrified her.

She wasn't sure why it was that this time around

she could see something almost tempting about such a freefall.

"So it's the dungeons for me, then?" And she really did try to keep her voice light.

"I cannot deny that I've enjoyed these weeks," Zago said, in that deliberate way he had. Yet his amber eyes had that gleam. And she could feel something prickle all over her skin, some kind of warning. "But then, this has always been the problem, has it not? Three years ago I assumed that the only way to contain this was to formalize it. You disagreed."

She actually laughed at that, because it was so unexpected. Like a sucker punch. "How funny." Irinka did not think it was funny at all, but still she kept laughing. "That is not how I remember it."

He had always been so good at this, she thought now. He could sit there as if someone was painting his portrait, a picture of dark masculine serenity, because that was what most people saw.

When all she could see was that simmering fury right there beneath the surface.

"What would you call it?" he asked, in a tone that suggested he was attempting to be reasonable. For her sake. As a gift.

It set her teeth on edge, but then, it was likely meant to.

"I don't see any point in talking about this," she said quietly, instead of succumbing to the lure of indignation. But he only looked at her, one arrogant brow raised high. And she had no doubt that he would keep her here, naked in his bed, until she had the conversation he thought they ought to have. That being the case, she decided there was no point in arguing. Better to fight with a weapon she had, she'd always thought. "If that's your recollection, there's no point arguing about it. Call it whatever you like."

That amber gaze of his was searing, then. "I am sorry that it is still such a burden to you to have a simple conversation. Three years have passed from the night you ran off without a backward glance. How silly of me to imagine that some maturity might have occurred in the meantime."

He intended that to be a blow, she could see that. And it was. She felt her temper surge in response, but she tamped it down. "If you think I am a silly little fool of a girl, the way you did back then, what purpose is there in having this conversation?" When he only glared back at her, she smiled wide, though it made her lips hurt. "I've never denied the chemistry between us. I was as overwhelmed by it as you were. But surely you understand that it was toxic."

"What I recall is that you told me you loved me, Irinka," he said, in that intense, low voice of his. "And that it was a lie."

The unfairness of that swept through her like some kind of dark tide.

It was a wonder that she stayed where she was, sitting up in his bed—the very same bed where she had lost her virginity to this man and experimented with sensuality and sex, love, and longing for the whole of that breathless, airless summer. He had taught her so much pleasure, so much joy, so much despair. She had felt something like *skinless* in his presence, so attuned to his every move, his every whisper, his every thought.

It was right here in this bed where she had learned that despite all of her mother's teachings over the years, she was actually fully capable of the deepest, wildest emotions.

It was also here, in this bed, where she had come to understand that if she did not leave this place and this man, she would *combust*. And there would be nothing left of her but ash.

And everything she'd ever been taught about the ways foolish women lost themselves in powerful men would have been for naught.

Even if she'd toyed with the idea, back then, that somehow she might be able to handle involving her heart the way Roksana had sternly counseled her never, ever to do. Not ever.

She could remember the exquisite grief of that summer vividly, knowing that she had only so much time before she would lose herself to the black hole of this passion that she knew even then could only eat them both alive.

Because that was what a passion like that did. Irinka was the result of such a passion herself, no matter what vile things the Duke liked to claim in the aftermath. She had known better.

But oh, how she had loved him. As well as she could, for as long as she could.

"You know perfectly well that it was no lie," she said now, and it was a grueling sort of effort not to give in to the urge to shout at him. He wanted that, she knew. Because it proved that what he said about her was true and it *wasn't*. "What you won't accept is that there was no way to control this. No matter how hard you tried. Making me into some perfect Venetian housewife couldn't have changed that."

"Baldisseras are not housewives," he retorted with a silken fury. "But even if they were, I fail to see the issue. I thought you took great pleasure in these roles you play."

"I might enjoy playing a role, it's true." And this time, the way her temper rose was different. It wasn't a combustible fire, or any kind of explosion. It was a slow kind of simmering thing. She didn't think it would eat her alive—she thought it might scald her if she didn't let it out. "What about you, Zago? No matter what act *I* put on, I always know the difference between the stage and me. Can you say the same?"

He stood then, though he did not move any closer. Not yet. "I don't know what you mean."

"Don't you?" She let her head tip to one side, but she didn't look away from him. "You hide away here in this half-ruined palace in a sinking city, telling yourself that what you're doing is building out your family's legacy. You can never measure up to the things your father claimed were required of the heir to all this because he made them impossible on purpose. Impossible duties. Unacceptable responsibilities. The weight of all that history and a moral code he did not live up to himself. And yet you can never make up for what your mother—"

"If I were you," Zago said, very, very quietly, "I would not speak about my mother."

"Why not?" Irinka asked him. Or dared him. "Isn't she the real reason this house is so haunted? Isn't she the reason that your father all but abandoned his own children? Why he decided that he could lose himself in your family's illustrious past, making up wilder and wilder stories as to why it was that he would need to live forever and—"

"I warned you."

Zago was moving then, crossing the room swiftly until he was there at the bedside. And so Irinka moved too, meeting him. Going up on her knees so that they were face-to-face.

So that he would see that this time she had no intention of backing down.

"You were the one who thought it sounded like a fine idea to tear into our past this morning," she pointed out. "Or is it only my past that you think needs interrogation?"

"Your past is complicated, is it not?" His voice was like ice, his eyes like chips of obsidian. "It is no wonder you walk around with a chip on your shoulder. You have been forced to carry the shame of your parents' affair, forced to answer their sins, all your life."

"I spent almost no time at all thinking about my parents' affair," Irinka said with a laugh that was not forced, exactly—but was also not precisely *organic*. "My mother has had a great many affairs, as it happens. I spent time considering precisely none of them."

"I don't believe you."

"That's all right," she replied, and her voice was something like soft now. Something like it, anyway. "Shame requires secrets. When a secret shame is in every paper, there's actually a ceiling on it. There is no further shame once that ceiling has been met." Irinka took a breath, and said the rest of it. "I'm not sure the same thing can be said about guilt. Especially the misplaced guilt of a son who thought he should have saved everyone in this family, but couldn't."

Including your sister, she wanted to say, but didn't quite dare.

She could see from the look on his face that he wanted to put his hands on her. There was a part of her that wanted that, too. Because maybe he'd forgotten this, in their years apart from each other. It wasn't that they hadn't talked the last time, it was that they hadn't had their discussions in *words* back then.

It had all been heat and disaster, wildfires and regrets.

Maybe it made it easier to mischaracterize people.

But he did not touch her then, despite the temper and heat in his dark amber gaze. And she couldn't tell if she wanted to celebrate him for that or mourn it.

"My mother was not like yours," he told her after a moment, all that old pain in his voice. And Irinka found herself holding her breath, wondering if he was actually going to talk about something she had only ever read about in anodyne news articles and taut little paragraphs of snide speculation. "She was a fragile, emotional creature. She was raised for sunlight and ballrooms, laughter and parties. And my father may have wished to grant her those things at some point, but he was a man burdened by his obsessions."

"I hesitate to point out that such a burden runs in your family," she said. "And in your case, involves kidnap."

She would not have dared to say something like that to him three years ago.

His eyes blazed. "I've talked to every servant who was in this house back then," he told her. "I have made it clear that it was only their honesty I was looking for, to gain some kind of perspective on events that occurred before my birth. So that I could better understand what happened later."

"You don't have to dig this up," she said then, because it hurt, and that was the part that she'd forgotten. That when this man hurt, she did, too. It was so unfair. And it made everything else that much harder.

"Venice is a city of graves," Zago told her darkly. "We float upon our ancestors and sink, in time, to meet them. The veil between these things is cracked, eroded, washed away. And my mother was not made to live in the in-between." His jaw worked. "Over time, she grew sadder, and I do not think there was any cure for it. But I also think that neither she nor my father thought to look for one."

There was no part of Irinka that wanted to have this conversation any longer. But she couldn't seem to stop herself from merely…kneeling there. Sitting back on her heels, studying his face, trying to understand him at last.

She couldn't pretend that wasn't what she was doing.

"And this is never something I would say to my sister," Zago told her, gruffly, "but it is a certainty that our mother did not recover after giving birth to her. She was already frail and a shadow of herself, and then…"

He trailed off and shook his head, his shoulders stiff as if even this was a responsibility he carried.

"Zago." Irinka said his name deliberately. She interlaced her fingers before her and held his gaze as best she could. "I didn't bring her up because I was trying to hurt you."

"Why not?" he threw back at her. "I should have expected it."

That felt like a low blow, so low it took her breath away. "Because I'm so terrible?"

"Because I did it first."

And that emboldened her, somehow. "I only meant that the way you look at what happened between us before doesn't take into account that, perhaps, neither one of us is well-equipped to handle that much emotion. That much…"

But she had never known what to call this. How to quantify it.

"Is that why you went out and became who you became?" Zago asked, quieter now. But that fire in his gaze still burned. "Did you really believe—*do* you really believe—that spending your life breaking up relationships for these cowardly men who cannot do it themselves was preferable to marrying me?"

She had not expected him to *say* it. Sometimes she thought she had imagined that part, there at the bitter end.

Sometimes it was easier to think she must have.

"Zago—"

His gaze gave her no quarter, then. "Or is it that you thought that marrying into this family was a death sentence?"

And she must have known that he would go there. Wasn't that where this conversation had always been heading? Wasn't this why they'd avoided it in the past?

Because Zago kept going. "Just as it was for my mother when she took her own life."

CHAPTER SIX

HE COULDN'T BELIEVE that he had actually asked that question. When he'd promised himself, time and again, that he would not. That it didn't matter.

That *why* was a fool's game and he had never been much for games. He'd never had the time to indulge himself in such frivolous pastimes.

And in any case, she hadn't married him. She had left him.

Those were the only facts that mattered.

But Irinka looked…winded. She sank back a little farther on her heels, as if she'd deflated, there before his eyes.

"That had nothing to do with it," she said after a moment. "I wouldn't say I was aware of all the ghosts here that summer. There was only you. And this. I'm not sure I thought about anything else until afterward."

"I find that hard to believe."

Meaning, he did not believe it at all. There were so many scandals and tragedies in Venice. Every ruined palazzo was a treasure trove of loss and pain, family secrets and shame. Sometimes he thought he'd like to make a map of the sorrows here that marked this city through the ages.

But he had only ever been intimately acquainted with *this* family and *this* palace.

And the woman who had run from him as if he was the ghost here, all along.

"Zago. You and I…" Irinka shook her head, her blue eyes clouded, then. "It wasn't healthy. Nothing that happened between us was *healthy*. It was over-whelming. It blotted out the sun. It was unsustainable and I don't understand why you don't see that."

"Anything is sustainable if you *try to* sustain it," he said, darkly.

She blew out a breath that sounded far too much like a sob. And he hated seeing anything but brightness in her gaze. "Imagine if you considered the possibility that everything I do or say is not designed to hurt you, Zago. What then?"

And he opened his mouth to immediately refute that, like some kind of knee-jerk reaction that wasn't his to countermand—

But he stopped himself.

A memory teased at the edges of his thoughts, then seemed to bloom into being. Some deathly-dull meal with his parents, long ago. He had only been a boy, though he had considered himself a man, and he had viewed these forced family moments as a torture designed deliberately to plague him.

As was his custom, he had tuned his parents out

completely, since they were given to their tedious discussions of the things he was certain *he* would never lower himself to care about, like politics and the weather and the opera.

But something in their tones caught at him and he'd lifted his head from his daydreams, focusing on the two of them for a change. There had been a shift.

His mother had sighed. His father had been frowning.

If it was something that could be fixed, I know you would fix it, his mother had said. *Like you do every other broken thing in this house.*

Zago had looked away again, assuming they were talking about the usual repairs or floods. It wasn't until many, many years later that the memory had come back to him and he'd thought to wonder if it had been a very different sort of conversation after all.

And then he'd had to wonder if his father's obsession with the family's history was his way of coping with what couldn't be cured in the present.

Even after his mother had died, his father had hidden himself away in the libraries, chasing down arcane little bits of fact and fable and painstakingly piecing it all together, as if a finely researched mosaic of the Baldissera past would redeem what had happened to him.

To all of them.

Was what he was doing here—to Irinka—really all that different?

She had offered him hope, that summer. That he

could do this differently. That he could navigate this life better than his parents had done if she was with him. That they could find their way, together.

Then she had taken that hope with her when she'd gone.

And so he had hunted her down. He had— happily—arranged for her to be bodily removed from London and brought here. He had insisted that it was all about Nicolosa and yet, behold—here was Irinka, naked in his bed.

Was he any less obsessed than his father, in the end?

Or any less sad than his mother?

That settled on him like the weight of a new palazzo, with all its history and legend, bills and renovations.

And Zago had always considered himself the most rational of men. He hadn't had any other choice, had he? Growing up in a house where his mother was so fragile, so often ill, and forever victim to the voices in her head, and his father retreated further and further into the past while leaving it to Zago to take charge of things.

Which he had.

How could he have done that if he was not all that was reasonable and rational?

But he was staring down at Irinka now. This woman who, little as he wished to admit it, had been haunting him for years now.

This woman who he had imagined was a terrible

party princess and an entitled brat. He'd been certain he could bring her here, put pressure on her, and expect her to crumble.

Instead, she had taken on her so-called Cinderella role with good humor and a surprising work ethic.

He could admit, now, that she'd shocked him.

And then there was what had happened between them since.

Zago couldn't pretend that he hadn't entertained the thought of what might happen between them if they were ever together again. But he hadn't truly believed that would happen. He had imagined that he would confront her here. Perhaps rake over the past. That he would find some grim satisfaction in that, or better still, find himself indifferent.

And instead, there was this.

There was Irinka in his bed again and the taste of her in his mouth. There was Irinka, kneeling there before him with her blue eyes wide, her hair a mess, and a distraught look on her face.

Not the expression of the shallow, selfish girl he'd imagined she was these past three years—and certainly this past month.

But then, did he really believe that she was the woman he'd decided she was in her absence? The woman he'd pretended she was, because that made it easy to dismiss what had happened between them, or cast himself the victim, or otherwise excuse himself from what had happened that summer?

When, as she had just said, it had been all-consuming between them, but it had not been *healthy*.

Zago wasn't sure he knew what *healthy* was.

Thinking these things made him feel a bit too much as if he was standing on shaky foundations. The same way her question had done.

What if you considered the possibility that everything I do or say is not designed to hurt you, Zago?

Maybe he was afraid that if he admitted any of that, if he allowed that question to alter him in any way, it would be worse.

But Zago had not lived a life that had ever allowed him to worry over much about the things that made him afraid. Whether he was afraid or not of something had very little to do with his actions.

He'd learned that here, too.

"Are you going to answer me?" she asked, and he realized he'd been standing there too long, all these things racing through his head.

So he blew out a breath and told himself that might clear his mind. He moved closer to her and really took in how she reacted. She didn't move. She didn't brace and she didn't flinch, which was, perhaps, a low bar.

Her eyes widened even more, however, and he wondered how he'd never noticed that she really seemed not to know that nothing on this earth could compel him to hurt her.

Not with his hands, anyway.

He climbed onto the bed next to her, then shifted

them both around until they were lying on their sides, looking at each other.

Though he noticed that she was holding her breath.

"All right, then," Zago said, trying this out. This new *consideration* she'd suggested. "You are not trying to hurt me. What happens now?"

Irinka looked startled. She blinked, and then, slowly, a smile began to take over her face. A benediction Zago had not realized he needed.

"I...don't know what happens now. I don't think I imagined it was possible that you would listen to me."

He reached over and pushed a hank of her black hair back, then tucked it behind her ear. "Am I really so overbearing?"

"Intense," she said. Still smiling. "Always so very intense."

"And you think that this intensity is inhibiting me in some way?"

She laughed, and then changed her expression, frowning thunderously. Then she made her voice deep when she spoke. "Of course not. Because here in this palazzo that has been in the Baldissera family from time immemorial, intensity alone keeps the stones from sinking beneath the waterline."

It took Zago a long, stunned moment to understand that she was mocking him. Teasing him, he amended. He didn't like it—

But in the next moment, when she smiled at him again, he decided that it was not so bad. It was not terrible to be the reason she smiled like that.

So he moved forward, and she did too, and it was so different to kiss like this. The sun beaming in. laughter between them, and none of that dark, driving need and desperation that colored every memory of every moment he'd ever had with her.

He felt like it was some kind of gift, that laughter. This moment. This kiss.

So he took his time moving his way down her body, spreading that heat. Losing himself in that fire.

Until he could settle himself between her legs, lick his way into her core, and set them to gleaming bright like the sun.

He was too conscious of the way they'd shifted. The magic of it, dancing within him, and he wanted to give that back to her. He dedicated himself to casting that spell.

Zago pressed incantations into her most tender places, encouraging her with the sounds he made low in his throat as he lifted her up toward the pinnacle, then backed away. Once. Again.

"I will kill you," she managed to cry out, her back arched and her arms over her head. "If you don't kill me first."

"No need to fling yourself into the abyss so quickly, Irinka," he murmured, smiling as he traced her soft heat with his fingers. "Martyrdom is so messy."

Then he bent his head to her once more.

And only when she was sobbing with pleasure did he crawl his way back up her body. He memorized her as he went, etching her into his bones.

Tattooing her every response, her every scent and taste, deep into his skin.

Exploring this light they made together with her, while he could.

She pushed him onto his back and he let her, sprawling out on the bed while she took a turn at making spells, letting her hair brush over him as she slid her way over his chest, his abdomen, then lower still to take the length of him deep into her mouth.

And he let her play with him, for a time. It was exquisite. It was too much.

It was Irinka. The agony and the longing and the glory. All her.

But he did not intend to end this in her mouth. Not this time.

When he could take no more, Zago pulled her back and laughed at the half crestfallen, half outraged look on her face.

"I wanted to—" she began, hotly.

"You can bear the tragedy, I promise," he told her.

And then he crawled over her and thrust deep within her, smiling as she broke into pieces. He held her as she shook and sobbed, and then, as she came back to him, he began to move.

Slow and steady, until she broke apart again. Then faster the next time.

Until she was moaning his name and he was something like feral, incapable of anything like control until he lost himself, too.

Only with her, he thought as he spun out into eternity, holding her tight. *Only Irinka.*

For a long while afterward, they lay there together, holding on to each other while their breath stayed wild.

Later, they sat together on the balcony and looked out at the *vaporettos* and *gondolas* going by on Grand Canal. He called down for food and Irinka seemed entertained to greet the friends she'd made among his staff when they served her.

"Bit of an upgrade," she murmured to them as the meal was laid out. "I rather think it's because of my excellent scrubbing of that front step."

And when the staff were unable to muffle their laughter, something that would have been unthinkable in any other circumstance, Zago reminded himself that it was not necessary for him to be *quite so* intense all the time, and allowed it.

He found it a particular pleasure to break bread with this woman. To talk of things that were not so emotional, or so personal. To share an anecdote or two, and not look for land mines in every sentence.

It reminded him of all those conversations he'd thought were boring when he was a child. Were they simply a bit of plaster over the cracks, smoothing out the bones of the place, a way to keep things humming along like this—all sunshine and a smile?

That felt like another revelation.

And so he was unprepared for it when Irinka turned to him at the end of the meal, the afternoon sun bathing her in a golden glow, and smiled ruefully. "You know I can't stay here," she said.

Zago was unprepared, and his first reaction was the searing shock of betrayal.

But there was something wise and knowing in those blue eyes of hers, as if she could see his reaction all over him. As if she was waiting for him to backtrack and start hurling accusations at her again, as if he hadn't learned a thing today.

He would obviously rather tear off his own head.

"This is gorgeous. Venice is like a dream and I'll even admit I didn't mind the hard labor." She smiled at that, inviting him to find the housework she'd called *hard labor* as amusing as she clearly did. "But I do have a life in London. I have commitments."

"That tasteless job of yours," he said, before he could think better of it.

"You and I will have to disagree about what it is I do," Irinka said, but not as if she was taking offense. "And I cannot compromise a client's privacy, of course, but I can tell you that there are no repeat clients on our roster who I would recommend as a love interest for anyone. Much less your sister."

There were a thousand things Zago wanted to say to that. He said none of them.

She nodded, though. As if he'd said enough. "I have been here for weeks now. Surely there can be no more reckoning required."

He wanted to tell her to apologize to Nicolosa, but he remembered something she had said at the start.

When she'd pointed out that he wasn't off pounding down Felipe De Osma's door, demanding apologies from *him*.

And the truth that was sitting on him strangely today, despite how rational he believed himself to be, was that the moment he'd seen Irinka's name he had thought of nothing else. Nothing and no one. "I will certainly point out to my sister that a man who would hire someone like you was never the man she thought he was in the first place."

"And never will be," Irinka said in soft agreement.

Then she sat there before him, an odd sort of look on her beautiful face, and it took him a moment to realize that she was waiting.

She was waiting for him to decide what it was that he would do now. She was giving him that space and he didn't know what to make of it.

Or, something in him whispered, *you do know.*

He thought of his poor, lost mother, who had never been able to get past her own broken heart and the twisting paths in her brain. He thought of his father, who had lost himself completely in his fantasy over what the past might have been, if only he could prove it.

He thought of his sister, who could not let go of a man she never should have dated in the first place.

And here he was, once again trying to hold on tight to someone who didn't want to stay.

Did it really matter why?

He already knew that if he dragged her back here,

they would end up the same place. The way they had this time. And he liked this place more than he should, but it was no different from that summer they'd shared.

Fleeting. Temporary.

Because he wanted things she either did not wish to give, or couldn't.

Maybe what he was having trouble with here was nothing more or less than the oldest story there was. A person, no matter their strength and power, will, or determination, could not make another do anything they did not wish to do.

Not really.

And did Zago truly want something he had to force?

He already knew the answer. Which was, he was certain, the reason he had never asked himself that question before.

And so, even though it made him feel as if he was cracking wide open and shattering in half, burning down like the front part of this palazzo once had and with less hope that there could be any kind of reconstruction, Zago Baldissera did the one thing he had never done in all his days.

He surrendered.

"Very well, then," he made himself say, perhaps more gravely than necessary, but it was all he was capable of when her smile was too knowing and the sun seemed to taunt him. "When will you leave?"

CHAPTER SEVEN

NEXT TO DREAMY, breathtaking Venice, London was a grim, gray sprawl of concrete and exhaust.

It was well into May now, and the weather was often pretty, but it still felt gloomy to Irinka. She walked to the Tube in the morning, paying no attention to the hints of spring flowers in boxes and gardens along the way. And it was often a bright, happy sort of evening on her walk home, but to her it might as well have been storming down pellets of rain on her head.

Maybe it was fairer to say she couldn't tell the difference.

There were clients to soothe in the wake of so many canceled appoints, each of them with a vast male ego that required she cater to them as if they were the only man alive—the sort of thing that Irinka normally did on autopilot. But she'd left that particular skill behind in the Grand Canal, it seemed.

Because try as she might, she couldn't seem to find the will to return those calls. She couldn't even listen to the usual outraged messages, because the sort of men she worked for were always ruffled and stroppy until they felt appropriately catered to, and she simply didn't have it in her to *murmur encouragingly* and make *assenting noises* until they decided they'd shouted long enough.

This was not a problem she'd ever had before.

It was almost as if she'd come back home as someone else.

One night Irinka walked back from Notting Hill Gate. She walked and walked, and only noticed that she'd sailed past her own front door when she found herself tramping about in North Kensington. The part of North Kensington that only dreamed it was Ladbroke Grove. When she finally noticed that she was taking herself on an impromptu walking tour, it was the better part of a half-hour's walk back to her own front door.

"So you took a holiday in Venice," Auggie said at a Work Wives lunch one day, purportedly so they could gather and discuss work, but mostly to celebrate the fact they were all back in London at the same time. A rare occurrence these days. "And yet you look like you need a holiday to recover from your holiday."

"Doesn't everyone?" Irinka asked dryly.

"Perhaps not quite so much of a holiday, then," Auggie murmured.

But Irinka ignored her. She tried to focus on the others, because she didn't need reminding that these sorts of nights were rare. Back at university, there had been nothing but time. Long nights piled into common rooms or loafing about in each other's rooms in halls. Dreaming up glorious futures at the local, dancing madly in the discos for each other's entertainment more than anything else. They'd plotted, planned, dreamed, and they'd done it together.

Irinka knew she wasn't the only one who viewed these friendships as something more like sisters, taking the place of many of their rather less congenial family relationships.

Or maybe that was just her.

And in any case, it would only get more rare to have the four of them together now.

Because her friends were happy. They were in love, and it was the kind of love that made each of them *better*. She could see it in the way they all…inhabited their own skin differently than they had before. Maude was talking about landscape architecture with a smile on her face. Lynna held forth on her strong opinion that pies should be savory, not sweet, but she was laughing as if she'd finally decided it was okay to be a little silly, if she liked.

It was Auggie who kept watching Irinka's face, as if she was that close to giving herself away. And the mad part was that Irinka couldn't tell. All her friends were more authentically themselves than ever, loved up and gleaming, and she felt as if she'd had to put on a costume to play the role of herself today.

Like all her bones had been rearranged in Venice and she still didn't know how they worked.

Auggie tuned back into the conversation, which

had something to do with Lynna's disdain for the pub's lofty menu and Maude's stinging critique of the herbaceous border and shrubs, which Auggie claimed meant they might need to ascend to a wine bar next time.

"Maybe we are no longer the sort of women who pile into a pub on a Friday and get the pints in," Auggie said.

"Let's not get ahead of ourselves," Maude said with a laugh.

And Irinka decided that the strange emptiness she was feeling was actually freedom.

Not everybody got to revisit a defining, disfiguring love affair that had altered her life once already. The real madness was imagining that she might come out of it unscathed, just because it had been less of a bitter, acrimonious ending this time.

Not everyone got to go back to the scene of the crime that had broken her heart and repair it.

Because she was absolutely repaired, she assured herself. Stitched up and made new.

She smiled when everyone looked her way and leaned in, dropping her voice. "Guess what scandalous, outrageous gossip I heard only yesterday about a selection of minor nobles we may or may not have met at university."

Irinka decided that the only thing that was required of her was to enjoy this lovely late evening in an outdoor pub garden that regrettably did not meet Maude's standards, gathered around the picnic table until well after dark.

And sitting there spinning stories for her friends felt right—like she was finally fitting back into her body, and her life.

"Why do you seem sad?" Auggie asked later, as she and Irinka broke away from the other two and headed toward a different Tube stop.

"I don't know what you mean."

Auggie laughed and bumped Irinka's shoulder with hers. "You forget, I was there when you came back from Venice that summer after university. You look like that again, pale and wobbly."

"I'm not the least bit wobbly." Irinka made herself smile. "I'm not even wearing treacherous heels."

"Repeatedly saying that you're not a thing when I can see with my own eyes that you are doesn't change it," Auggie observed.

Irinka stopped walking and faced her friend, waiting for a rumbling double-decker coach to go by. "I appreciate that you're looking out for me," she said quietly. "Really. But I'm fine. You don't need to save me from anything. Not even myself."

Auggie gazed back at her, but a bit too shrewdly for Irinka's taste. "You do know," she said, almost carefully, "that the great mystery of Irinka Scott-Day might be why you get attention wherever you go, but it isn't why *we* love you, right?"

Irinka thought she would have preferred if Auggie had taken out a dagger and stabbed her straight through the heart. It hurt to smile, but she made herself do it.

"It's been a lovely night," she said. She gave her friend a hug, and she meant it, but then she turned and strode off, leaving Auggie standing there.

No doubt burning holes into her back with her glare, but that was better than carrying on with that conversation.

Irinka was grateful when she made it back to Notting Hill, and did not wander off in a daze this time. She made her way through the throngs crowding in along the Portobello Road, reveling in the mild weather and the hints of the summer ahead.

She wanted to find that kind of hopefulness. She wanted to tilt her head back and spin around, or do whatever it was *actually* free and unfettered people did in these circumstances.

But instead, she walked to her door and looked around—a bit longingly—to see if there were any black SUVs lingering at the curb, dispatched on strict orders to redo her kidnap. There were none. Only the usual drunks singing in the streets and the sound of traffic in the distance.

Feeling let down all over again, Irinka let herself inside.

She'd loved this little house on sight. It was one of the smallest terraced houses in this stretch of the road and like many of the others, had been falling apart until the 1980s or so, and was now valued at an extraordinary price. Buying it had felt the way she thought freedom should, because it was the first place that was entirely her own. Not one of her mother's flats or house shares, and happily purchased with her father's court-mandated settlement to make her love it even more.

Irinka thought that keeping the double-barreled surname that forever linked her to him, shaming him every time she signed her name or was mentioned in a news item, had been a lovely punishment for the Duke. But she also enjoyed living off his begrudging support, too.

A better person would be humiliated to take forced charity, the Duke had said to her once.

You mean, like the rest of your children? Irinka had replied. *Thanks, Dad.*

And over the years, she'd taken great delight in making the little house her own. She loved that it was small, suitable for only one person if that person truly wished to be comfortable. Or possibly a couple, if that couple got along well. There was room for guests, but only the sort who did not intend to stay too long.

Because Irinka had made every room hers.

She bought art from the stalls in the Portobello Market. She liked to haunt the galleries in Notting Hill, finding things she liked from emerging artists. Whenever she traveled, she liked to pick something up wherever she landed, so that the house was an eclectic mix of all the things that made her happy.

But tonight she stood just inside her door, breathing in *her space* the way she liked to do, and it hit her that it was all just...*things*.

She didn't know why she'd never noticed that before. She had a lot of stuff, but it was just that. *Stuff.* No different from all the statuary scattered about the palazzo in Venice.

But Irinka was absolutely not thinking about Zago.

Back in her kitchen, she set about toasting some bread, slathering it with butter and a bit of Marmite. Then she took her plate and a cup of tea up through the house to the tiny little rooftop deck that was half the reason she'd bought the house.

She sat outside in her favorite chair, crunching on her toast and waiting for a sense of peace to take her over, but it didn't come.

Instead, she could see Zago's dark amber gaze on the day she'd left. She'd promised herself that she would walk away from him without looking back, and she'd made it down that long, stone path. She'd worn the clothes she'd come in, though without her mobile stuck in her boot this time. And with every step, she'd assured herself that she was doing the right thing.

The *only* thing.

She'd climbed into the water taxi that he'd called for her, and that was when she'd looked back.

Like she wanted to give Orpheus a run for his money, she'd turned and looked.

Zago had been standing on that balcony again, his hands braced on the rail, his face expressionless.

But she'd felt the burn of his gaze like a torch.

It still woke her at night.

And even now, she felt heavy. Out of sorts, which she could admit was just another form of *wobbly.*

Maybe the real truth was that she'd expected Zago to fight her when she'd told him she wanted to go.

Up on the roof of her little house, Irinka blew out a breath at that.

But at least that was better than a sob.

That same sob that was lodged there behind her ribs like a bruise that never healed.

Irinka decided that she'd had enough of sitting out there as the night grew colder and London clanged all around her. She finished her tea and then she went back inside. It was odd to walk around her little house now, suddenly overly sensitive to all her *things*, so she tried to shower it off. And the city with it.

Then, still strangely wound up and in no mood to sleep when she knew exactly what would greet her once she crossed over into dreams, she called her mother.

"What is it?" Roksana demanded, not bothering with a greeting. Irinka wasn't sure she'd even heard a ring. "What has happened?"

"Hello, *momochka*," Irinka said ruefully, already rolling her eyes, because of course she should have expected this reaction. Roksana was always primed for disaster. "Nothing's happened. I just…wanted to hear your voice."

There was a pause. Irinka could imagine her mother rising from her bed in her current flat, a modern eyesore of edges and angles and low-slung cubes masquerading as furniture, all courtesy of her latest lover. This one was much younger than her and liked it when Roksana treated him as if he was a naughty puppy.

"At this hour, even I do not wish to hear my voice," Roksana said after a moment.

This was sentimental for her mother, Irinka knew. It was practically a good cry and a long hug, when most of Irinka's childhood had been arranged around various ways to toughen her up.

Irinka already regretted the impulse. "I'm sorry. I don't know what came over me. I wouldn't want to disturb your beauty sleep."

Back when she'd been young, messing with Roksana's rest had been akin to starting a war. But while her mother still prized her sleep, she was no longer quite so militant.

"Is this a call to merely…catch up?" Her mother sounded baffled. "Have you been at the vodka? Remember what I have always told you. Vodka spoils everything—"

"But the glass," Irinka finished for her. She sighed, frowning up at her ceiling. "You do know that some daughters call their mothers as a regular thing, don't you. They actually like to talk to each other on the phone. They're more like friends, really."

"I did not raise you to have friends." Roksana's voice was cool and untroubled. Irinka could hear her moving around her sterile flat with its commanding views, and wondered if that was happiness. Maybe she'd been getting it wrong all this time. "I raised you to survive under any circumstances, as I have done."

"But are you happy?" she dared to ask.

Roksana went quiet. So quiet that Irinka lifted her mobile away from her ear to make certain the call had not dropped.

"Are you at risk of bodily harm?" her mother asked after a long pause. "Do you need rescuing? Otherwise there should be no such calls."

"I don't know whether to take that as a vote for or against happiness."

Roksana sighed. "If you chase two hares you will end up with neither," she said. Her way of saying that a person couldn't have their cake and eat it, too. "Sleep, Irinka."

But after her mother rang off, Irinka did not sleep. She found herself thinking a little too much instead, as if her ceiling had transformed itself into a cinema where she could watch what had happened between her and Zago like a film.

She had asked Zago to look at things between them differently, and he had.

Why did she keep coming back to the conclusion that she should have done the same?

Irinka couldn't answer that. But as she lay there she accepted that leaving him was, in many ways, worse this time. Three years ago she had been so torn apart, so shredded into pieces, that she'd had no choice but to throw herself into absolutely anything that would take her mind off of Venice. That palazzo.

Zago himself.

She was certain that had contributed hugely to her zeal in setting up His Girl Friday with her friends and how she'd managed to round up clients relatively quickly.

But this time around, the thought of storming into anything—much less her client list—made her feel... sordid.

"This too shall pass," she told herself, and to lull herself to sleep, she decided she would watch nothing but frivolous things until she drifted off to sleep.

A few weeks more of that and she thought she might explode.

"Are you still in the doldrums?" Auggie asked when they ran into each other at the office one day.

A run-in that Irinka suspected Auggie must have planned, because Irinka had gone out of her way to choose a time when no one else was meant to be there.

"I've never met a doldrum in my life," Irinka told her as cheerfully as possible. "I exude happiness, Auggie. Is that not clear?"

"What's his name?" Auggie asked quietly.

And Irinka felt strung out on some kind of precipice, then. She hadn't spoken about Zago, ever. Not to anyone.

Because if she did, wouldn't that make it real?

And once it was real, how was she meant to survive it? She hadn't had an answer for that three years ago. She didn't have an answer now.

But it was clear that *not* speaking about him hadn't exactly been helpful thus far.

And maybe her friend had meant it when she'd said that it wasn't Irinka's mysterious side that she loved. That all her friends loved.

She didn't have to believe that to *wish* it was true. And maybe she was weak after all, soft in all the ways she'd been taught not to be, because she went with it.

"His name is Zago Baldissera," she heard herself say, almost as if someone else had possessed her body to spit out that name.

Auggie blinked. Then she started typing into her mobile and, a moment later, swiveled the screen around so that Irinka was staring directly at a picture of Zago himself.

Zago crossing Saint Mark's Square in Venice, the basilica rising up behind him. He looked like a dream. A dream she often had, and in far greater detail than this photo.

She sighed. "That's him."

And then sat there feeling as if her skin was trying to crawl off her bones as Auggie started reading out facts about Zago.

"Ancient Venetian family. Extraordinary family fortune. A palazzo, no less." She set her phone down on the desk between them. "Back then, too?"

Irinka didn't pretend to misunderstand her. "Back then, too."

"That was your summer of travel." Auggie frowned as if she was trying to think back those three years. "I don't even remember the names of those girls you were meant to travel with, off on some sort of Grand Tour."

Irinka did, and named them. "We all went to the opera in Venice. That's where I met him. When they moved on toward Croatia, I…stayed."

She and Auggie sat with that a moment, all the unsaid things that could be packed into that word. Into *staying*.

"And you went back last month. All these years later." Auggie frowned. "Why now? What changed?"

Irinka smiled. "That was more of an invitation that couldn't be refused. What I told you about the brother of a woman who I was hired to brush off is true. It was his sister. I didn't recognize her, but then, I really never have paid much attention to the women in those scenarios."

"The women in those scenarios weren't paying us," Auggie said, pragmatically.

"Funnily enough that was my argument, too."

And then Irinka found herself sitting there telling Auggie the entire story of Zago and her, even including her weeks of drudgery.

"You *cleaned his house*?" Auggie asked, her eyes round.

"I am nothing if not committed to a role," Irinka said loftily. "And I rather fancied myself a Cinderella, if I'm honest."

"And now you're here." Her friend crossed her arms and eyed her with something that looked a little too much like pity. "Irinka. You cleaned the man's house out of some form of malicious compliance because you knew that would get under his skin. You're sad when you leave him. Last time you built up an entire career arranged around reliving your breakup. Now you can't even bear to do it."

"That…is not how I would put it."

"Is it untrue?" When Irinka couldn't claim that it was, Auggie nodded. "Then what are you doing in London?"

And that was how, the very next day, Irinka booked herself on a flight and went back to Venice.

Of her own volition, this time.

Once she landed, she found herself a water taxi and had it deliver her straight onto the dock of the palazzo. She marched up the stone path she'd scrubbed on her hands and knees and presented herself at the grand door, smiling at Roderigo when he opened it.

"*La signorina* has returned," he said, not unkindly. But not in a particularly welcoming manner, either. "But without an invitation, I fear."

Irinka, who did not consider herself particularly impulsive, had actually not considered this part of her impromptu visit. And she should have.

"Will he see me?" she asked.

Because it didn't occur to her until then that he might not.

So she stood at the bottom of the steps, staring

back out at the canal and the boats. She soaked in the impossible splendor of this magical place, this floating city that seemed more dream than reality. She paid attention to the curious way that sound carried, dancing where it shouldn't and finding ways to sink in so unexpectedly.

And when she thought she heard a faint noise behind her, she turned and he was there.

Zago.

Somehow even more beautiful than when she'd left.

He gazed at her for a long moment, and everything was that amber, that fire. Then he looked past her, out at the water, and it shocked her how much that felt like grief.

After a moment he came down the steps and stood there—near her but not touching her.

Irinka wondered what a picture this made for the tourists passing on the *vaporettos*, the two of them standing there so awkwardly at the front of an ancient palazzo surrounded by June gardens and polished stone.

It almost made her feel as if she was a part of the sweep of history that sang its way up out of the stones in this place. As if this was all another way of claiming that what burned between them still was destiny.

Almost.

Because wasn't *destiny* just another word for surrendering to the things that refused to allow you to control them?

"You don't seem happy to see me," she said when she began to worry that she was, in fact, going to turn to stone where she stood.

"Should I be?"

And when Zago turned to look at her then, his amber eyes were blazing hot and that brooding intensity of his seemed to wrap itself around her as surely as if he'd put his hands on her body.

But he didn't.

There was something almost like sadness on his face, she thought then. Or maybe it was resignation. Whatever it was, it made something in the center of her chest go hollow, then seem to become its own, terrible drum.

"Have you come to stay?" Zago asked her, his voice that silken threat. "For good?"

She balked at that, she couldn't help it, and he saw it. Irinka watched his eyes track the movement, then shutter.

"For good?" she repeated.

And out there in all that golden light, he reached over and fit his hand to her cheek as he had before. As he had many times before.

It made that hollow drum inside her seem to stretch tight, then shiver into something else. Something she couldn't name.

"Letting you go gives me no pleasure," he told her in that dark, low voice. "And I want to welcome you in. But Irinka, there will be no more playing games. When you come back, *if* you come back, there will be no more half-measures. It's all or nothing. Are you ready for that?"

He waited, but everything inside of her seemed to seize, then shudder. Hard.

And she couldn't seem to make her own mouth open.

She couldn't seem to do anything but stare.

"That's what I thought." His thumb stroked her cheekbone.

Once, then again.

And then she stood there, stricken straight through, while Zago climbed the stairs and then closed that grand door behind him.

Leaving her there on the stones with a hollowness where her heart should have been and no earthly idea what she should do next.

CHAPTER EIGHT

ZAGO REGRETTED THE decision to turn Irinka away immediately.

He closed the door with great finality but then stood there on the other side of it, cursing himself. Cursing the weakness that still allowed her to haunt him like this, whether she turned up at the palazzo or stayed in London.

Because one place she always was, night and day, was in his head.

But he did not turn around, throw open the door again, and welcome her in, because he'd meant what he'd said to her.

That night he barely slept, certain that he had made the greatest mistake of his life—but then, that was every night. He had to believe that sooner or later, he would get used to it.

Sooner or later, he would stop worrying about how a man could live a whole life without his own heart.

Yet by dawn it was clear to him that the only thing he needed to learn to live with was his surpassing weakness. Because he knew as he watched the sun bloom into being, caressing the ruined old buildings and illuminating the water outside, that if she came back again this day, he would not have the fortitude to deny her entry once again.

But Irinka didn't come.

"And there is your answer," he told himself darkly that following night, as he lay awake in that bed that he might as well go ahead and burn, now. Because it was little more than an altar to his memories of her.

It might as well have been a mausoleum.

When he drifted off to sleep, he kept thinking that he caught her scent—like she was just out of reach on the same mattress—and he would spring awake to find her and touch her, but he was always alone.

And there came a point where he could no longer bear being a ghost inside his own home, like all the rest who were trapped in the old walls. Yet it was as if the ancient, floating city itself—murmuring and sighing all around him—was trying its level best to make him feel as haunted as possible.

Venice was ever a city of echoes. Ghosts were noisy here, and the dead were never truly buried. It was the easiest thing in the world to turn down the wrong, narrow lane and find a part of the city he didn't know.

It is like falling in love with a woman, his father had told him on one of their rare walks through the old city on a pretty evening, when Zago had still been young and both of his parents had still been here and he had not understood, yet, how drastically things could change. *She is ever-changing. She is always herself, always a mystery, unknowable and eternal. This city must be the love of your life and to love her, you must lose her and find her, again and again, a thousand times a day.*

Zago hoped he never grew too old or too bitter to enjoy the simple things in life, like following an echo wherever it led and then wandering the streets of Venice until he found his way back home.

He threw himself into the routines of his daily life as a lifelong resident and the scion of an ancient family, who had spent many years deeply involved in the local community. It was already summer and the cruise liners came in daily, hunkering over the city and discharging their hordes into the Piazza San Marco. Like most Venetians, he supported tourism insofar as it kept the city alive, yet grew weary of the summer hordes.

Still, he walked to have his morning espresso in cafés that were not in guidebooks. It was important to meet with friends and neighbors, have a coffee, and ground himself in the world of the living again. To speak again of art and literature and local politics.

To remind himself that there was more to his life than a woman who had left him.

Twice.

But the ghosts would not leave him alone.

It was a few days after Irinka had turned up at his door—and had been turned away with a great strength of will he was still surprised he'd had in him—when he caught, out of the corner of his eye, the figure of a woman.

Zago lost track of the story his friend was telling him in an animated fashion, leaning against the side of a high-top table. He looked again, and then shook his head, not certain why he had reacted so strongly to a mere glimpse of this woman. A closer examination only baffled him more.

It was not Irinka. It was a different woman entirely, blonder, huskier. Older.

And yet the sighting left him almost winded.

He even dreamed about it that night, the blonde woman changing into Irinka as he watched, then melting off into the bright sun outside…

"You sound strange," his sister told him when he made his daily call to her the following day. She laughed. "Stranger than usual, I mean."

"I beg your pardon," he protested, but mildly, because he hadn't heard her laugh in some while. "That is no way to speak to your revered and beloved older brother."

"Sometimes, Zago, I think you are a ghost yourself," Nicolosa told him, and though she laughed again then, it did not make him quite as happy as before.

Because how could he tell her that he was haunted entirely by his own hand?

A few days later, Zago left the crowded tourist areas behind, making his way through the snarl of lanes and bridges that led into the part of Venice that was largely without signs. A person either knew their way here, or they did not.

This was one reason that the farther he walked, the fewer people were about.

It was late into the evening, the lamps aglow and the sky still flirting with the last of its blue. He was heading into one of the neighborhoods only locals tended to know about and one of his favorite *osterias* to meet up with friends, enjoying the particular joy of Venice in the evening, The canals and the hints of music and laughter, dancing down the alleys.

Zago was halfway over a small bridge when the sound of a footstep behind him echoed strangely. He glanced back in time to see the side of a woman's head as she retreated back into the shadows of the alley he'd just come through. And he knew immediately it wasn't Irinka.

This woman had short hair and was dressed like an American tourist, in torn jeans and dirty sneakers, and she was swallowed up by the darkness before he could look at her straight on.

There was no reason that he should think twice about it.

But that night, sitting in a loud, happy group of friends he'd had since childhood, Zago found himself thinking about that American again and again. For one thing, tourists did not usually make it that far away from the bright piazza and famous bridges, the *gelaterias* and mask shops. And certainly not alone.

And for another, she had to have been following

him, or he would have passed her on the bridge. There was no other way to get to that particular alley.

Zago couldn't shake the odd notion that she had retreated back into the mouth of that alley when he'd turned to look at her.

And later that night, he found himself pacing in his bedchamber, wondering if he was losing it. If these odd sightings of strange women were a sign that his weakness was more mental than emotional. If he was destined to tear out his own hair and become one more ghost story the enterprising storytellers of this city would use to titillate the visitors on their nightly spooky tours.

But apart from finding himself fixated on strangers, he felt relentlessly the same. His work was the same. He tended to the accounts, he supervised the endless and ongoing maintenance of the palazzo, and he made certain that the financial portion of the family legacy was self-sustaining and would outlive them all. He allowed himself more access to *la bella vita*, as all Italians should.

His only trouble was that he kept thinking he saw Irinka everywhere.

Once more near an ancient church, its small square thick with guided tours and ill-behaved children, though she turned out to be a hugely pregnant woman. And again, standing on a bridge as his boat passed beneath it, half her face obscured with a camera— though something about her jawline lingered.

"If you'll forgive my saying so, *il padrone*,"

Roderigo intoned one afternoon, "you have seemed rather on edge of late."

"I feel on edge," Zago agreed, closing his laptop and standing. He accepted the espresso that the older man set before him with a nod. "Tell me, Roderigo. Are you worried that I'm losing my grasp on reality?"

His *maggiordomo* slid a look his way, his face almost too blank. "I am now," he said.

"I cannot be the only man who sees ghosts in Venice," Zago said, perhaps more to himself. "Though I know that we will all become ghosts ourselves, if the water has its way."

"I prefer to do without a haunting, if at all possible," Roderigo said, sounding only slightly reproving—but that was a comfort. Even now, when he spoke of Zago's mother, it was with that same gentle kindness that he remembered from back then. If Roderigo had been at all concerned about Zago, he would not be *reproving* at all.

The older man picked up the small cup and saucer after Zago tossed back the espresso. "This is already a city of too many masks, is it not? A ghost seems like overkill."

Zago didn't think much more about that conversation. The days grew warmer, the city more crowded, but also more musical and less haunted than it seemed in the darker months, where melancholy seemed to float along the canals like memories and barges.

He thought he caught the sound of Irinka's laughter on the breeze one fine morning, but when he turned, reluctantly, there was no one nearby—save an old woman and the birds she was feeding on the other side of the narrow waterway.

A few nights later, he made his way through the city at dusk, picking his way through the crowds waiting outside overpriced restaurants and eying glass beads through shop windows. He was heading for an art gallery not far from the Piazza San Marco and decided that tonight he was determined to be on guard against the tricks his memory intended to play on him.

No ghosts, he told himself sternly.

When he got there, the gallery was loud and full. Zago knew many of the guests, as well as the patron and the artist herself.

He took his time with the exhibit, lingering on each work to really take it in, and then it happened. As he moved from one grand canvas to the next, he thought he saw a particular smile flash just beyond the nearest pillar.

So much for his *no ghosts* rule.

Zago was tired of himself. He kept his eyes trained on the canvas before him, a lavish painting of one of Venice's masked balls.

And he thought about what Roderigo had said a few days ago. That theirs was a city of masks. That these masks allowed intimates to move amongst each other, unseen. Every family in Venice had stories about masks and balls and the particular delights of being anonymous in this place where they were all known too well.

Every Venetian child was raised on these stories.

And then, perhaps inevitably, he thought about Irinka. But this time he found himself considering that job of hers. The tasks she performed for those clients of hers.

And the fact that she billed herself as a master of disguise.

Those disguises were how she was never recognized. They were how she could pretend to be the girlfriend or wife or long-term mistress of any man at all, and was always believed.

She can dress up as anything or anyone, one of her happy repeat clients had told Zago with great admiration. *I reckon she could pass you on the street and you'd never know her.*

His pulse was pounding through him.

Irinka.

It had been Irinka all along.

Zago turned, slowly and with all apparent ease, but he did not look toward the pillar where he had last seen her. She would not be so foolish. He would have caught her already if she was that kind of foolish.

He ambled through the gallery, smiling and nodding at all the familiar faces. He had a drink, told a story, laughed with his acquaintances.

But all the while he was scanning the room. Not for the black hair and blue eyes he knew so well, but for other tells that she could not hide so easily. Her height, or someone hunched over to pretend she was shorter—he thought again about the old woman and the birds the other morning—and that was how he found her.

Once he knew what he was looking for, it was easy.

She was hiding by standing out tonight in a blazing red wig in loose, tumbling curls. And he thought from this distance that her eyes were green, suggesting that contacts were involved, and the kind of heavy cosmetics he had never seen on *his* Irinka.

But it went further than that. He was not a poetic man and yet Zago felt that he could easily write a book of sonnets concerning her particular lithe, lean form. The woman with the red hair, by contrast, was voluptuous. Padding, he assumed.

None of that mattered. He knew it was her.

He could make out those cheekbones he liked to trace with his fingers. He could see the mouth he had kissed too many times to count.

And then there was her smile. He would know it anywhere.

He knew it now.

Zago pretended not to notice her at all. Instead he tracked her movements through the gallery, waiting for an opening. For the right moment.

It came later, after the artist thanked everyone for coming and there were toasts and applause, and the voluptuous redhead who was no ghost after all slipped out the side door, clearly thinking that no one was watching her.

He followed, tracing her into the shadows as she moved from the art gallery, and then wound her way down one crowded, narrow little alleyway into another, before she burst out into the Piazza San Marco itself where the famous clock tower stood watch and the Basilica gleamed in the dark.

It was a mild and pretty summer night. The restaurants were full, orchestras dueled, performers wandered, and the crowds were replete with pasta and gelato and the sea air. Irinka slowed as she wound her way into the thick of it and let the packs of tourists carry her along.

Zago was glad of it. It allowed him to track her all the better. And as he did, he could see that any tension in her body eased away as she let the hordes of people direct her this way and that, no doubt imagining she was in the clear.

Because she always had been before.

She navigated her way across the square toward the Basilica, then ducked around it, back into alleys and byways that led her along a canal off the piazza. Zago knew immediately that she was heading for one of the hotels on the other side.

So he lengthened his stride and caught up to her right there on the crest of the bridge that arched up over the canal. By day there would be a steady stream of people here, moving from one neighborhood to another. But tonight it was only them, a gondolier singing lustily into the night, and the simple satisfaction of the way his hand closed over her wrist at last and tugged her around to face him.

"Can I help you?" she asked boldly as she looked up at him, complete with an Irish accent.

"I told you not to come back unless you planned to stay," he reminded her, filled with that pulse that hammered at him and the silken menace that was taking him over. "And instead you have taken it as a personal project to turn yourself into a hundred different women, then haunt me in every corner of my life." She looked as if she was about to argue that, so he tugged her closer, or maybe he simply leaned down into that face that was all hers and not hers at once. "Did it not occur to you that I might worry that the ghosts I kept seeing were an indication that the family madness had reached me, too?"

He saw her eyes change at that, even though they were the wrong color. "I did not think about that," she admitted. She blew out a breath. Then, more quietly, she said, "I'm sorry. That wasn't my intention."

"You will have to explain to me what your intentions were, I think." The gondolier moved around the corner, heading deeper into the stillness and night. They were alone, now, in this pocket of quiet, as if the city floated only for them. "Was this a punishment in kind? You thought you would haunt me for the great sin of turning you away? When you have already left me twice?"

If he had imagined he would confront her with calm rationality, well. That was as unavailable to him as the gondolier, now only a faint melody in the distance.

"I don't know," Irinka said, and she hardly sounded like herself. Her voice seemed too high-pitched, as if something had changed inside her. As if she wasn't quite the woman that he remembered, and he wanted to take some kind of joy in that.

But he didn't believe it.

Because these were still games and he was tired of playing them.

"Irinka." And her name still tasted like a song on his lips. "I told you exactly how you can come back to me. It is simple enough. But it cannot happen in costume and deceit, clambering about in alleyways pretending to be someone else."

She did not look anything like herself and yet his chest hurt when she looked away, off toward the Bridge of Sighs in the distance, not quite visible from here.

"You say you want everything," she said, then. Softly. "But that's not true. You want total capitulation. You want me to come crawling to you."

"I cannot imagine you crawling." He turned her wrist over in his grip, tracing the delicate skin on the inside, where her pulse beat like his. "Then again, I did not imagine that you would take to the streets of Venice in costume, your very own Carnival."

She looked down at the way he was holding her wrist, and he thought he felt her tremble.

"I don't understand," she said quietly, and it was becoming something like an out-of-body experience to hear her voice coming out of the wrong woman. As if she was presenting him with the essential issue between them with her disguise—the Irinka he longed for and the woman she pretended she was. He could touch them both, but only one of them was real.

What Zago did not know was *which one* that was.

Irinka lifted her head to look at him, then, her distractingly green eyes solemn. "You say one thing, and I think you believe it, but the truth is that you don't want *everything*. No one ever does. So where does it leave me if it turns out that I am a whole lot more than you bargained for?"

He moved closer and lifted her hand as if to put it to her face, but dropped it again. "I can't look at you while you're dressed like someone else. It's disturbing."

She made a frustrated kind of sound at that. Then she flipped her wrist so she could tug him along with her as she continued across the bridge, and he let her do it.

Because despite what he'd told her, he didn't know what he wanted. He was outraged, obviously. But there was also a part of him that couldn't help but like the fact that she hadn't left Venice. That she had stayed all this time, and had stayed close.

Irinka led him off the bridge and then directly into one of the hotels that waited there on the other side, built on the canal. She swept inside, waved at the dazzled man at the desk, and brought him up a narrow set of stairs to a hotel room with casement windows that opened up over the bridge below.

Once the door was closed behind them, she pulled off the wig and tossed it onto a table, where he could see many other bits and pieces of disguises. Torn jeans. Blond hair. She shot him a look and then strode off into what he assumed was a bathroom.

And when she came out again, she was herself.

His Irinka.

And that was both worse and better, all at once.

"Tell me what you want," he demanded. She looked haunted, and something like furious, and he didn't know what to do with that. He didn't know what to do with any of this. "If you wish to haunt me, tell me why. Because otherwise it feels like torture, Irinka."

"I thought it would be entertaining," she said and she smiled, somewhat self-deprecatingly. "More fool me."

He moved toward her then, something wild inside of him that was clawing at the inside of his chest. He backed her up until they moved straight out onto a tiny balcony overlooking the canal, the lights of San Marco in the distance.

But there was only the real Venice here, secrets and sighs, and he could not help but indulge himself.

He knew better, but he pulled her into his arms and then swept her back so he could kiss her. Again and again, as if to assure himself that he hadn't made this up. That he hadn't been driving himself mad.

That she really had been here in Venice the whole time.

He kissed her and he kissed her and when he

thought he might lose control, he set her back on her feet. She gazed at him, her properly blue eyes blurry, and she looked dazed and soft.

And Zago had never wanted anything more than to pick her up in his arms, carry her inside to lay her on that bed inside, and lose himself in her.

But he knew too well that losing himself like that was losing her for good.

So he did not pick her up again. And he kept his hands on her shoulders until she could stand without swaying.

Then he waited until she looked at him. He held her gaze, and didn't recognize his own voice when he spoke. "If you want to come back, come back. Don't pretend."

Her lips parted, and she looked at him as if he'd said something terrible.

Or painful.

"But…" She shook her head, then pressed her lips together. There was a suspicious sheen in her eyes. "But what if pretending is the only thing I know how to do?"

CHAPTER NINE

ONCE AGAIN, IRINKA felt skinless.

Exposed and naked, though she had clothes on.

Not that silly dress with all the padding built in that had made her look like some kind of silver screen goddess. But an old T-shirt and a pair of lounging pants that she'd thrown on in something like a panic, half-convinced that by the time she came out of the bathroom—no longer in any sort of disguise—he would have left.

She wasn't sure she would blame him if he had done so.

Instead, he had kissed her on the balcony. It should have been swooningly romantic, wildly hot and beautiful, and it had been.

Everything with Zago was all of those things.

But somehow, Irinka wanted to cry. She wanted to dissolve into that sobbing thing that still camped out there in her chest, threatening to spill over at any moment.

She almost wished that it would.

Zago stared down at her, his gorgeous face carved

into something stern—but the light in his amber gaze felt like hope. She told herself it was, because it had to be.

Though the truth was, she didn't have the slightest idea what it was she ought to hope for here. All the possibilities seemed designed to take her breath away, and not necessarily in a good way...

"It is very easy to stop pretending," Zago told her with that *certainty* of his that made her bones feel like melting. Like it was an imposition for them to hold her upright. "You simply...stop."

Irinka actually laughed at that, and the sound of her own laughter reminded her that they were still standing out on the balcony. And more, that Venice was an echo chamber at the best of times, but especially at night. Stiffly, waiting for her bones to betray her, she moved inside.

And felt out of sorts all the while, as if she thought her body might mount its own revolution at any moment. She sat, gingerly, on the end of her hotel bed, not entirely certain that her own limbs would obey her.

Then she found herself gazing up at Zago as he stood in the windowed doorway to the balcony and studied her where she sat, his expression unreadable.

"I don't know that I've ever seen you so uncomfortable," he said after the moments seemed to expand into separate eternities. "Is it that much of a trial to simply be yourself?"

"You seem to have no trouble with it." It felt like

much-needed action, to throw it back on him and see how he fielded a question that made her whole body ache. "How do you go about it?"

His lips curved, but it didn't look like a happy sort of smile. "By now you must realize that I was born with a destiny, a set of immovable expectations, and very clear directions on how to achieve all of the above." Then, as if he was quoting someone, "Bald-isseras are not merely born, but carefully and deliberately bred."

"I never thought your childhood sounded quite so structured." But Irinka considered that a moment. Had he actually talked to her at any length about his childhood? Or had she made assumptions based on what had happened to his parents later—and then filled it in with what she imagined it must have been like to live in the same place for an entire life? "Then again, it is not as if you speak about it that much."

"There are two versions of my childhood and the older I get, the more I realize that both are equally true. And equally false." Zago shook his head, that same bittersweet curve to his lips. "In one, it was a magical time. I explored the palazzo, and this city of myth and memory, as I chose. What is not to like about such a life?" He tipped his head slightly to one side, as if that was a trick question. "And in another, I was tutored from a very young age to think more of a ruined old building on its rickety foundations than any of the people I encountered. To place it above all else, and do whatever was necessary to restore it or revive it, as needed. And in the midst of all of that, of course, there were the usual expectations of a man in my station. The kind of education it was expected I would procure, to be a credit to my name. The kind of people I am expected to know and maintain relationships with throughout my life, because we are all rotting away here together."

His amber gaze seemed to blaze straight through her. "I have never gotten the impression that your childhood was bucolic and sweet in any regard."

And maybe she was going to have to get used to the fact that she felt winded in his presence.

"I knew I was a bastard before I knew what it meant," Irinka told him quietly, and without realizing she'd intended to say such a thing. It was as if it welled up from that same space inside of her where that un-sobbed ache still *hurt*. "I used to tell my mother's friends what I was at parties as it always got a big reaction. In some circles, it still does."

Zago's expression shifted in a way that made everything inside her list a bit to the side, like she really was melting in on herself. He moved into the room and crossed to the bed, and Irinka thought for a brief, dizzyingly sweet moment that he was simply going to pull her into his arms and kiss her senseless again. Or bear her back down onto the bed and make all of this simply swirl away into all the bright colors they made together, the way he always did.

The way she desperately wished he would.

Instead, he came and stood before her for a moment, then squatted down so he was almost at her eye level. She had to look down at him, just slightly.

"You are not pretending now," he pointed out in that measured way that she wanted to rail against, even as it felt like some kind of caress. "How does it feel?"

"It feels silly that we both have our clothes on," she replied.

She expected to see that heat in his gaze. Was banking on it, in fact.

And so there was nothing in her that was prepared for the way that sad smile took over the whole of his beautiful face, making her worry that once that ache inside of her let go, there would be nothing left of her. Not one shred or scrap or shattered little piece. That it would all swirl away into the mess of those tears she was afraid to cry.

Her heart was pounding so hard that she was shocked she couldn't hear it echo back at her from across the canal. "Whatever you might think of the costumes and all the rest, you know as well as I do that at least *that* has always been real between you and me, Zago. You know that it is."

He didn't dispute that, but it was no comfort. "You have been hiding since the day I met you," he said, very distinctly.

She felt something in her shaking, like her body was trying to tear itself apart from the inside. "I met you at an opera. I was in the stalls like everyone else. You were the one in the box, hiding."

"I met you at the café in the interval," he corrected her. "And if I had to guess, I would say it was your first time at an Italian opera, that you didn't understand a word, but you happily assumed the role of an opera patron anyway. And the thing is, Irinka, you're very, very good at it."

"And what…you think I was pretending that whole summer?" Her throat was on fire. Irinka was tempted to imagine that she was coming down with some terrible fever, but she suspected she only wished that she was.

Because, unfortunately, she was not feverish at all. She was frozen solid, incapable of movement, and yet hanging on his every word even while she wished that he would stop.

"I think that at first, you were overwhelmed," he told her, and there was something inevitable about this. As if she had known that he would say these things and had avoided any circumstance in which he might. "And then, as best as you could, I think you were pretending that you could really do it. That you could stay with me. Marry me. Live with me ever after, even though it all happened so quickly. So unexpectedly."

Her lips felt chapped. Her throat was aflame. "It was a love affair. Affairs end."

"How would you know?" And that dark amber gaze of his was like fire. "You have only had the one, spread out over the course of all these years. And last I checked, *tesoro mio*, you couldn't let go of it yourself. You settled in, changed your appearance, and held on tight. So what do we call a thing that does not end?"

She moved then, as if to reach out for him—

But he caught her wrist and held it there, between them.

"No," he said, and that he sounded almost *kind* did not help. It made that feverish thing all over her seem to burn all the brighter. "I meant what I told you on the steps of the palazzo. It is all or nothing."

"Yet you accuse *me* of playing games," she managed to say, while everything in her seemed to be going haywire. She couldn't *breathe*. Her heart actually hurt where it beat inside of her. And she simultaneously wanted to melt into the grip he had on her wrist and tear it away from him, because if he wouldn't give her what she wanted—

But it was too tempting to get angry when it wouldn't solve anything, only delay it. And she doubted it would help her, anyway.

"I have had a lot of time to think about you," he told her, with that same disarming, disquieting intensity. "That summer. The three years after. The month I spent fuming over my sister's disappointment. And all the time since I brought you back here, up to and including the little haunting you have treated me to these past weeks. When I take myself out of the equation, it all seems obvious." There was something like laughter in his eyes, when she had never felt less like laughing in all her days. "I know you like to think of yourself as deeply mysterious, Irinka. But in the end, you're not."

She tried to swallow past the fire in her throat. "I suppose I can comfort myself with the knowledge that you can apparently read me like a book, yet keep reading."

"I think your childhood was not kind to you," he said in that darkly quiet way, as if she hadn't spoken at all. "I don't think there were any different versions of it to confuse the issue or pretty it up. Your mother, for all her beauty and success, is a harsh woman. Famously so. Your father was prepared to put you and the rest of his family through hell to keep from owning up to the reality of the fact that you were his. How could these things not take a toll?"

This time she did pull her wrist away from him, and then held it in her lap as if it was burned. "I've always wanted therapy. I thought it would be so soothing, so lovely and sweet, to sit about on comfortable couches and talk about my troubles. Another notion disabused."

He did not rise from where he squatted before her, and he did not move that intense gaze of his from her face. "I think you learned how to be whoever you have to be, Irinka. I think you can change the versions of yourself at will and as needed, and you do. That summer, I think you felt deeply vulnerable for the first time in your life and you hated it, so you decided to make a profession out of it. Because no one could accuse you of playing games when it was your job, could they?"

Irinka stood up then, in a blind rush. She moved away from the bed, jerkily, skirting his body and putting space between them until she found herself standing there near the table where she'd arranged all the different disguises that she'd used while wandering around after him. And she couldn't tell if she felt foolish, indignant, terrified, or all of the above.

And still her heart kept up that calamitous beating. And still, her whole body felt singed to a crisp, inside and out.

"You talk a lot about playing games," she managed to say, and even managed to keep her own voice even and low. As if this wasn't wrecking her the way it was. "But I seem to recall that you're the one who had me picked up off of the street in London, transported across Europe, then dropped down into a choice between sexual favors or domestic labor."

"Perhaps I was trying to speak to you in a language you understand."

She looked back at him over her shoulder. "I don't think you were."

He stood then, too, and they faced each other with the floor between them, but still not nearly enough air. "You're right. That's the thing, Irinka. No one is entirely in control of themselves or entirely aware of the reasons they do things, not every hour of every day. But, to be clear, I never thought you would take either one of those options. I suspected that you would not be too scared—"

"By a kidnapping? That's quite an expectation."

"—which is why I sent an entirely female crew to collect you. To help assuage any doubt."

"You are too kind, Zago. As always."

Irinka wanted to rage at him. To throw things. To turn this all around and use it like a weapon but she didn't have the appetite for it. She kept feeling that everything was lost already, and possibly always had been, and the harder she tried to hold on to it the further away it got.

It was a lot like panic, now that she thought about it.

"What I thought," he said, in that steady way that only seemed to poke at that panic, and make it worse, "was that it would force an honest conversation with you that I felt was three years overdue."

"I've always been honest with you," she blurted out, because that felt like an attack.

But he didn't reply. Instead, he looked past her to the table piled high with all the various disguises she'd worn.

Irinka felt herself flush, and worse, felt a wave of something too much like shame wash through her, staining her. Inside and out.

"I'll tell you once more," Zago said with that quiet finality. "All or nothing, Irinka. And this time, I do not want to see versions of you out of the corner of my eye every time I turn around."

"You seem very certain of my response," she said, and her heart was going so fast and so hard that she was terrified that at any moment it would slam straight into that trapped sob, and then she would be in pieces.

At which point, she thought she might simply collapse, because she couldn't see past it. She couldn't see anything behind that pulsing ache in the center of her chest.

And all he did was raise a dark brow, so there was nothing to see but searing amber and calm query.

"Am I incorrect?" And there was a darker current in his voice, then. "I'm delighted to hear it. You wish to gather up your life in London, set it aside, and move here for good? You wish to live with me in the palazzo, marry me and have my babies, and lie beside me every night as long as we both live? What a glorious day. Shall we mark it as our anniversary, do you think?"

She put out her hands, hardly understanding what she was doing. "Stop," she whispered. "Please, Zago. *Stop.* I have to think."

"No," he corrected her, and though there was a dark fury in him, his voice was quiet. "You do not have to think. You would *prefer* to think, because that is what you do. You think up barriers, you think up long absences, you think up disguises and subterfuge. You don't need to *think* a thing, Irinka. You just hope that if you do, you can get your brain to tell your heart that it's a liar."

She felt a great trembling come from deep inside of her. It felt cataclysmic, as if her bones were trying to separate from themselves, and at any moment she might simply—

"If you're so bloody *certain* about everything, I don't understand why you don't just say so," she threw at him. "I don't understand why you didn't say so from the start."

"Because you can't handle it," he bit out at her, that dark fury more obvious now, and that did not feel like the victory she'd expected. "I was foolish enough to think that we both understood what was happening that first time and that even when you left Venice that summer, you would be back. I was wrong. And you're right that the way I brought you back into my orbit was its own kind of game. But now I am forced to think that if I hadn't done it, it would never have happened. I would never have seen you again."

Her breath *hurt*. "I would be glad of that."

That, too, did not have the effect she expected. All Zago did was shake his head.

A great deal as if he despaired of her, and that made her feel bruised all over.

"Irinka." Her name sounded like a curse. "You maddening, impossible woman. *You are the love of my life*."

And he did not wait for her to absorb that. He seemed to know it was a blow, or maybe he didn't care, because he laughed in that way he did when he didn't find anything funny at all.

"Do you think that pleases me?" he demanded. "Do you think that three years ago, when you were moments out of university, heedless and reckless, I was looking for this kind of mess? Do you think you were what I had in mind as the next Baldissera wife? The mother of the heirs to my family legacy, who must shepherd it long into the future? But there you were. Standing there in La Fenice and it was over the moment our eyes met."

Irinka remembered that moment with perfect clarity, as if it had only just happened. She had been transported and though she hadn't been fluent in Italian then—and was only slightly further along now—that hadn't been required to fall in love with it. The opera was timeless, universal. She had been floating on air when she and her friends spilled out in the interval to join the crowd at the café on the third floor.

She couldn't remember what she'd ordered or if she'd ever gotten it, but she remembered turning, her head wild with the music as if she was half-drunk on it, and there he was.

It had been like falling off of a great height, and perhaps the real truth was, she was still falling.

"I'll admit that there was an instant connection—" she began.

"It was love at first sight, and you know it," he threw at her, and it wasn't that he was loud, it was that she could feel the intent behind each word, as if he was hammering each one directly into her heart.

"You have always known. You know it now, little as you wish to admit it."

Irinka felt torn asunder. The cataclysm inside of her was ongoing and she could not understand how it was possible that she might survive this moment. There was so much tearing, so much cracking and shattering, that she expected her body to simply implode into ash at any moment.

Yet somehow she was still standing. She couldn't make sense of it.

"I don't understand why we can't go on as we are," she managed to say. "It doesn't require all of these wild declarations, surely. There's no need for them. We don't have to *declare* anything, we can just—"

"Tesoro mio," he said, and that endearment—again—stopped her cold. He came toward her and his gaze was intent, a dark amber blaze. His mouth was a grim line. "Until you believe that you deserve more, you will never, ever have it. And until then, Irinka, you will also never have me."

He was close then and she thought that when he leaned in it was going to be one of those terrible, glorious kisses—

But instead he traced the line of her cheekbone, that gaze of his stamping into her, leaving impressions behind that she wasn't certain she would ever get out.

And in the next moment, he was gone.

Irinka heard the door to her hotel room close. Or she thought she did, somewhere over the clamor of her heart.

And inside, still, everything was shifting, changing, *hurting*.

Without conscious thought, she rushed to her balcony and gripped the rail as she looked down at the canal below.

In a few moments, Zago appeared below and she watched the fine lines of his gorgeous form as he strode up and over the bridge.

She ordered him, silently, to turn around to look up at her. She begged him to look back, but he didn't.

He didn't even pause.

Zago swept over the bridge and then disappeared into the dark embrace of the Venetian alleyway on the other side, as if he had never been here at all.

And it struck her hard, like a blow to the back of her head. All deadly force and no quarter given.

Irinka staggered back, his words like a litany inside her head, competing with the rattle and thump of her heart against her ribs.

She looked around at the hotel room. At Venice out her window and the pile of disguises that she had taken so much pride in, because so highly did she rate her ability to disappear.

It was love at first sight, he had said. *And you know it.*

And it felt like an accusation. It felt like a punishment.

That terrible sob in her chest began to grow, that ache sharpening so much she almost thought it might kill her, and maybe she wished it would—

But then it burst.

And for the first time in as long as she could remember, since she was a very little girl and in all honesty she couldn't remember it even then, Irinka sank down onto the floor, buried her head in her hands, and cried.

CHAPTER TEN

THIS TIME, WHEN Irinka went back to England, she did not wallow.

She did not waft about London, trying to match the Big Smoke in all its gray sprawl.

And that was handy, because it was a lovely summer. Bright and clear—and that meant there was no pretending that she wasn't, in fact, the great cloud currently storming her way all over the British Isles.

She spent her first night home in her little house in Notting Hill, but everything seemed different to her now. Had she collected all of these things because she truly liked them? Or because she'd liked thinking up a different persona to go with each purchase?

Because she could remember each and every one of them as if they were friends, not parts she'd played. At the same time, she could remember how it felt to play each character, how soothing it was to slip into a different skin, and see the world out of different eyes.

Just as she could remember all the time she'd always liked to spend here, alone, reacquainting herself with those characters. As if she was always auditioning to see which one might fit the new moment she was in.

Irinka had always viewed it as her secret weapon, this ability to become someone else when it suited her.

But now she found herself wondering if what she'd actually been doing her whole life was trying on characters, waiting to see if one fit. Changing roles with every new person to lessen the possibility that anyone might get fed up with her and discard her.

No wonder her own skin felt so strange.

She didn't call her friends. She did check her voice mail and wasn't entirely surprised to find a series of increasingly unhinged messages from her clients. Though she would have preferred to ignore work entirely, she decided that the last thing she needed was these men in her life any longer.

So she called each and every one of them and noted that they were all confounded when she did not lapse off into character—the flirtier, sweeter, more amenable character she usually played for them—while talking to them.

"I don't know what you expect me to do," said one man, who'd had Irinka staging scenes to break up with a girlfriend for him for the past two and a half years. On a strict seasonal schedule.

"The way I see it, you have two options, Craig," she told him calmly. "You could stop dating women that you don't like, thereby skirting the necessity to get rid of them every three months. Or—and this might come as a shock—you could also break up each one of them yourself. Like a man."

And perhaps there was something wrong with her that she found herself smiling at his outraged, sputtering response.

But she held that closely, like a personal security blanket, as she went and got on the train. And then sat back, staring out the window as the train slowly heaved itself out of London proper, and on into the countryside.

It only took a bit more than a quarter of an hour before she found herself in the old market town and decided—it being such a lovely day, summery and blue but not too warm—to walk out along the hedgerows into the rambling, wildly green land that made up this part of the countryside.

She had always wanted to walk here.

And so she did, enjoying the feel of the sun on her face and the way her body responded to the motion. Her feet on the ground, her arms pumping.

No characters, just her.

Irinka turned in at an old stile, climbing up and over it, and then followed a path that rambled along until it turned into a bit of a lane. She wandered past a selection of lakes, one complete with its own dramatic folly, before walking up a drive rich in ancient oaks whose branches created a dense green canopy overhead.

And when she got to the top, an imposing stately house sat there. The way it had been sitting there, proud behind its gates and deep in the heart of all this beautiful land, for centuries now.

There were flags flying at the top of the house, because, just like royalty, the Duke always wished the common folk to know when he was in residence. Not so that they would think to call upon him, but so that they would know better than to trouble him at all.

Irinka had no such qualms. She marched herself right up the formidable front steps and rang the actual bell that graced the epically grand front door.

Then smiled at the dour-faced butler who answered.

Eventually.

Really, she was becoming an old hand at presenting herself at the doors of historic old houses and demanding entrance.

"His Grace is not accepting visitors," the butler told her, with scandalized affront, to make it clear that it was not the done thing to simply *appear* at the door of a house like this. As if she was a tinker selling her grubby wares.

She only smiled wider. "Luckily enough, I am not a visitor. I am His Grace's disgraced and illegitimate daughter."

The butler was unmoved and, in any case, she suspected he knew exactly who she was. It was his job to know such things.

So Irinka shrugged. "If he does not wish to see me, I will simply call the first tabloid that comes to mind and see if they can provide a more sympathetic ear."

And as she'd known it would, that got her ushered right in. The butler stalked off into the bowels of the house and Irinka followed. When she'd been younger, as much as she'd disliked her father, she'd found herself wondering what it might have been like to grow up in a place like this. So crushed beneath the weight of its own self-importance that even the ceilings seemed to hang lower than they should.

But now she thought of Venice. She remembered the airy rooms of the palazzo, always opened to the world of water and wishes that was just outside. And now as she walked through the Duke's ancestral home, all she could wonder was how many ghosts lingered in these hallways—and how lucky she was that she'd never spent enough time here to see them.

Because the mean old ghost she saw when she came here was always the same one.

And, tragically, he was still alive and what passed for well. Or so she assumed, because surely someone would have told her if he wasn't. And she knew perfectly well she would be swept back up in the news coverage once he died.

Something else to look forward to, she told herself tartly as she walked down the hushed corridor decorated with medieval suits of armor on podiums every few feet and ancient banners from old wars proudly displayed.

The butler led her to the same room that she was always led to when she came here. Or was brought here, the way she had been long ago. He opened the door, looked at her as if she was a deep, personal insult to him and this house, and then waved her inside.

Where the Duke, her father despite how arduously he wished to deny it, stood in front of his vast and important desk, vibrating with rage.

At least she assumed it was rage. It wasn't as if she'd ever seen a different expression aimed in her direction, and every time she saw him, she was forced to reflect that it wasn't the best look on a man so red of face. And with a belly that made her think that perhaps he was too committed to his puddings, and likely plagued by gout.

She considered it a sign of great personal growth that she wasn't even *tempted* to say such things to him.

"Hello, Dad," she said instead, and yes, she was fully aware that he would probably have preferred to discuss his ailments than listen to her call him *Dad*.

Irinka had planned this all out on the way back from Venice. After she'd picked herself up off the floor sometime much later that same night. And then had soaked herself in her bath for so long that she thought she'd never unpickle herself. Once she'd dried off, she'd collapsed into bed and had passed out into an exhausted, dreamless sleep.

In the morning, she'd begun plotting out her next move.

But this time, she had no intention of playing her usual games. She winced at the word. This time, she had particular questions she wanted to ask, that was all. And she intended to get answers.

Even from the Duke.

Yet before she could launch into the things she wanted to ask, her father took the opportunity to speak instead. Jowls trembling to indicate that he was appalled by her, as usual.

"I knew you would come crawling back," he spat at her. "I suppose you've blown through all the money I already gave you, haven't you? I told you then that I won't be footing the bill for your lavish, irresponsible lifestyle. I've paid, and I won't pay more."

Irinka stood there, gazing at him. Looking at him the way she would any person she might encounter on the street and not coloring the experience with the clips she'd seen of him and her mother when they'd been dating. Not weighting it down with the fact he'd fathered her.

What she saw was an old, sad, unhealthy man who thought his wealth would save him from everything that irked him, even death. Maybe especially death.

"I'm very well," she said quietly, after a moment. "Thank you so much for asking."

"You have spent your life skating about on my good name," he frothed at her, his brows practically tangled together, his frown was so deep. "Embarrassing my family with your shamelessness."

"Oh, no, Your Grace," Irinka replied in the same quiet tone. "I'm afraid they do that all by themselves."

And it was tempting to remind him that his heir

was a gambler, his spare was an addict, and his daughter was on her third divorce, but she was certain he knew that. Just as she was certain that somehow, he would find a way to blame her for it.

"I won't give you a single sodding pound," the old man told her, his voice trembling. "If you ran through your settlement, that's on you. I can only hope that you and your mother *finally* descend into the sewer from whence you came."

And Irinka couldn't decide if what she felt as she stood there before him was temper or sadness. It was a kind of grief, that she was sure of, but she couldn't quite put her finger on what kind.

Because she didn't want a relationship with this man. She had only meant to ask him why he'd thought it was necessary to be so cruel to an innocent girl who had nothing at all to do with what had happened between him and Roksana. She had wondered if now, all these years later, there might at the very least be a frank discussion.

But instead there was this. The same as always.

It wasn't that she was surprised. This was the man she'd met when she was a girl. This was the man who had revealed himself in all of those tabloids, and in court, as small and mean. Over and over again.

Maybe she had been hoping that in the fullness of time, there could be something other than vitriol between them.

"Do you have nothing to say for yourself?" he demanded. "After all the fine schools I paid for?"

"I had quite a lot to say, actually," Irinka replied, thinking that she would have been better off having this conversation with one of the empty suits of armor outside. She would have gotten more back. "But now I don't really see the point of it. I don't want your money."

He scoffed. "A likely tale."

"I think you are confusing me for every other person in your life," Irinka said gently. "I'm sure you will be delighted to know that I not only have *not* run through the funds you provided me so generously when ordered to by the court, but have significantly expanded my portfolio since then. No thanks to you."

His face began to mottle, so she smiled. "I would rather sleep rough than take anything else from you, ever. I wanted only to ask you a question, daughter to father. But I suppose you've answered it, haven't you?"

"You can see yourself out," the Duke snarled at her. "And don't come back."

Irinka shook her head. "I don't think you have to worry about that."

And it was the strangest thing, but as she walked away, out of the gloomy halls of his old house and into all that waiting sunshine, she felt as if a set of weights she hadn't known were strapped to her came loose. She could almost imagine they were floating off like rogue balloons, and no doubt getting trapped in the eaves.

But it didn't matter where they went. They weren't hers any longer.

She took that long walk back into town, and took her time with it. Then she sat and waited for the train, understanding that this time, she really wouldn't be returning.

This time, she really was done with everything involving that man.

Except, of course, his good name.

Irinka laughed about that all the way back into London.

And once there, she didn't head toward her little house again. Instead she made her way over to her mother's current flat in a desperately chic and outrageously expensive block of them on the Thames. She announced herself in the lobby and then took the dark, metallic elevator up high. She was not surprised to find her mother waiting for her when the elevator opened directly into that sleek, dramatic living room, the low-slung mid-century modern pieces disappearing against the view of London from every vast window.

In the midst of all that, Roksana looked like a goddess.

Perhaps that was the point.

"Now we are dropping by?" her mother demanded. "Without even a call?"

She was as brusque as ever, but Irinka noticed that she came closer as she spoke. Her gaze moved all over her daughter's body, as if she was looking for signs of damage.

"I have some questions for you," Irinka said, when it looked as if Roksana was slightly mollified not to find any blood or obvious bruising. "I think I've been waiting to ask them all my life."

"Beware a question whose answer must be excavated to be known," Roksana intoned. "I would sooner take my chances with wolves."

Another question Irinka wanted to ask her mother, but not now, was why wolves featured so significantly in her conversation when as far as Irinka knew, her mother had never encountered one. Nor the woods she often claimed was their home.

But that wasn't why she was here. "Do you love me, *momochka*?"

Roksana flinched, as if Irinka had taken a swing and punched her straight in the face.

"What is this question?" She sounded cross, but Irinka had seen that flinch with her own eyes. "Have you taken ill?"

"I know you won't answer me," Irinka said. "But I wanted to ask anyway."

She looked at her mother and, as always, it was like looking into her future. The same black hair. The same blue eyes. Irinka had always thought her mother was more beautiful because of the way her face was sculpted into near otherworldliness, though she knew some people considered that a kind of hardness.

They had the same build. At different points, they'd

shared the same clothes. People had often said they looked like sisters, and Irinka had never found that insulting. How could she? Roksana was still considered one of the most beautiful women on the planet.

Besides, her mother had only been eighteen when she'd had Irinka. She had already been famous for years. And Irinka had read many articles that claimed that a fame like Roksana's meant she wasn't any sort of typical teenager. That she'd had been *wise beyond her years*, which was the thing that men always said to excuse the fact that *they* were apparently too immature for theirs.

Roksana had been told by everyone who mattered that her career would be over if she had her baby, much less kept it. Irinka knew that she had always taken great pleasure in proving them wrong.

"Of course I love you," her mother said, belting the words out as if she thought that if they lingered on her tongue, they might bite her. "Can this be in any doubt?"

"What about all of your lovers over the years?" Irinka asked. "Did you love them, too?"

She had made a pact with herself long ago only to remember the ones she liked. Mats, the Viking, who had made them all laugh so much. Olivier, the great reader, who still sent Irinka book recommendations from time to time. Byron, whose sweetness had seemed like a miracle to her in the midst of a rather bruising few years there.

Roksana looked at her for a long moment and then

she turned, making her way across the vast living space. She paced across the room like it was a runway and managed to look the part despite wearing the most casual of clothes, and then settled herself dramatically in the chair she preferred, likely because it resembled a throne.

She picked up the drink that she'd left there. There was a time when Irinka might have investigated to see if it was vodka or not, but that didn't matter now. Her mother could do as she liked. She had earned that.

Surely they all had.

"I think you must tell me why you are asking me these things," Roksana said, in a neutral tone. That was her mother at her most suspicious.

"These aren't questions meant to trap you." Irinka trailed after her mother, and sat down on one of the low couches. "I honestly want to know. The thing is, I don't…" It was so hard to say out loud, even to Roksana, who made a habit out of not reacting to anything. It had always made her a safe space, really. "I don't know how to love anybody. I think I've been pretending."

"Don't be silly," her mother said at once. "You have those friends of yours." She swirled her drink around in its tumbler. "I have always been impressed that you were able to do this, Irinka. Have these friendships and maintain them. This is not something that was available to me."

"Was it not available to you or did you not know how to do it?" Irinka asked.

Roksana looked out toward that endless view over London for a moment, though Irinka didn't think she was examining Big Ben in the distance. She took her time looking back again.

"I was terrified to bring a daughter into this world," she said, in a voice very different from the one she normally used, so brusque and harsh. Roksana sounded…hushed. Irinka would have thought her *uncertain*, but that was not a state she could imagine her mother inhabiting. Not even for her. "I already knew what it was like to be a girl and I could not recommend the experience. I learned many things too young. And I did not want you to have to figure out how to survive those things as you went along, so I did my best to make you tough. If you started tough, you would not have to learn toughness the hard way, by surviving." She did not smile. She looked at Irinka, her gaze stark and direct. Blue to blue. "I did what I thought was necessary to keep you safe."

What she did not say, because everyone else who had seen them always said it for her, was that she had understood that Irinka was beautiful. Just as she had been. And she'd understood that their kind of beauty was as much a burden as it was a boon.

Roksana had made sure she'd comprehended that young.

Your face is so lovely that the rest of you must be sharp, like a knife, she had told Irinka when she was very young. So it would sink in early and stay.

And Irinka really did love her mother, despite the

things she'd done, and hurdles she'd made her daughter jump over, time and again. She really did love this woman who she knew, with every fiber of her being, would have died for her a hundred times over.

Sometimes she thought that's what Roksana's court case against the Duke had been about. She'd had her own money. She hadn't needed his.

But she didn't like the way he'd felt he could talk about her daughter.

Roksana might not have been a tender parent. She was not cuddly. Irinka had heard her say, more than once, that she was not tactile and that had extended to her child.

But her love was fierce and dangerous. Her love was like a weapon, and Irinka had always known that it was hers whenever she might need it.

So she did not tell Roksana that some of the ways she'd made her daughter tough had broken her where it counted.

Because maybe that was her own fault, in the end. There was a certain point that everyone had to take responsibility for their own lives, wasn't there?

It was love at first sight, Zago had told her, and his voice still rumbled around inside her. Like thunder.

Irinka went over and hugged her mother. And then held on, even though she knew Roksana hated it. Because even though she did hate it, and stiffened at first, Roksana eventually relaxed. With a sigh.

And patted Irinka on the back. Again and again, until she let go.

"There," Roksana said, looking somewhat wild-eyed, as if she had passed a treacherous test of some kind. "All is well, yes?"

"I love you, *momochka*," Irinka murmured.

Then she kissed her on the cheek, and left.

She thought a lot about her friends that evening when she was tucked up in her house with a take-away. And the fact that a woman like Roksana, who trusted no one and was proud of that, had noticed that Irinka's friendships were real. And good.

A glance at the text chain showed that her friends had moved on to a rousing conversation about the potentially dueling weddings they were all planning.

Irinka joined in, presenting them with hastily assembled mood boards designed to make each one of them scream in horrified laughter, and found herself laughing too, sitting cross-legged on the cozy sofa in her living room as she sent them all a barrage of images.

Each one more outrageous than the last.

When she looked around and saw all the characters she'd played up there on her walls, she realized that she'd forgotten to include her friends in all of this *reckoning* she was doing.

These women who had loved her no matter what state she was in, or what character she was playing. These women who had supported her, and laughed with her, and were never afraid to tease her or call her on her nonsense.

These friends who allowed her space and always welcomed her back as if she'd never been away.

These friends who asked for nothing but her, however she showed up. In whatever role she was playing that day.

How could she say that she didn't know love, when *of course* she did?

How could she think that she didn't have the slightest idea how to have a relationship, when she'd been having four rather deep and consuming ones all this time? Individual relationships with each one of her friends, and then the group relationship they all had together?

Why did she think that love only mattered when it involved a man?

She had to sit with that one some while.

And eventually, it led her around to her job. And how she'd researched all the details in each case, but had never spent any time figuring out who the woman was in each instance whose heart she was pummeling with her antics.

It wasn't that she thought she was *more* responsible for the way those men had handled their relationships than they were.

But she also had to wonder why it was she'd never given a second thought to any of those women.

Except one. And only because her brother had insisted she think about her actions.

And that was how she got the bright idea to go find Nicolosa Baldissera and apologize to her.

Not only because she was Zago's little sister, but because she was representative of all the women that Irinka had believed she was saving. When, maybe, she was more like Roksana than she wanted to admit—and her version of saving a person was harsher than she wanted to admit.

Maybe she'd learned that cruelty was kindness a long time ago and had never had occasion to question it until now.

"But now," she told herself as she left her house that evening, "you are questioning *everything*."

It had been easy enough to find the younger girl. Because it was easy enough—if a person had a particular set of skills and access to certain databases—to locate the properties owned by her brother, look them all up, and then determine which one she thought would appeal to a younger university student.

Then it was nothing at all to turn up at the lobby of Nicolosa's building, pretend to be one of her friends, and have the very nice security man—who probably should have been less forthcoming, and likely needed someone to tell him that, though it wouldn't be her—tell her in a chatty sort of way that Miss Baldissera had popped out for dinner.

"Over the road at the brasserie," he confided. "If I heard it correctly."

Irinka smiled. "I'm sure you did."

She walked back outside and decided that she felt different as she made her way down to the zebra crossing, then over the road. It was a pretty night and the light was lingering. The air was cool, and even though she thought that ought to have felt gray straight through after all the revelations she'd had since Venice, she didn't.

Maybe she couldn't.

There was a freedom in confronting both of her parents, choosing what to take and what to leave. There was a freedom in acknowledging that she didn't know how to love, and hadn't, for years now. Not the way she wanted to.

Not the way Zago did.

She had to think that there would be a freedom in this, too. In acknowledging the role she had played in another person's life. No matter what her intentions might have been, she had contributed to someone else's pain, and she wanted to acknowledge it.

And she didn't think about what her reception would be or what it might accomplish. She knew she needed to do this and she wasn't thinking about the future. She wasn't tallying up these revelations, like she thought a certain amount of one thing or another would help her find her way back to a man with dark amber eyes in a flooded city.

The future would do what it would.

That, too, felt like a freedom.

Irinka walked into the brasserie, not surprised to find it high-end and crowded. She smiled at the maître d' as she walked past him. She looked around, certain that she would be able to recognize Nicolosa based on the pictures she'd seen online.

Maybe she was a little bit embarrassed that she couldn't remember her from that night in Felipe De Osma's flat.

But she saw Zago instead.

And she froze.

He was seated at a table with a pretty young girl, and she knew immediately that it was his sister. Something she probably would have guessed even if they didn't look so much alike, and she hadn't just been examining Nicolosa's pictures online.

But there was that moment first.

That split second when the pit of her stomach opened and it was like concrete dropped straight through, making her feel sick and dizzy at once.

And she understood in that moment how little she'd really grasped about the service she'd been performing.

Irinka stood there, watching Zago and his sister talk. She saw him smile engagingly, and tease an answering smile back.

And it was like a key into a lock.

The bolt was thrown, and now she understood at last.

It was a wonder that it had taken her this long. But, by the same token, if events hadn't happened in the precise sequence they had, she knew she never would have gotten here at all. She would likely have been in a new costume, haunting this very restaurant.

"May I help you, madam?" asked the maître d' from beside her.

And when Irinka turned, she made sure to keep her back to the table until she was sure she was out of sight, smiling at the man as she went.

"I was looking for someone," she told him. "But I think... I think I must have gotten it wrong."

Deeply and surpassingly wrong, she told herself when she pushed her way outside.

She took a deep breath when she hit the street, filling up her lungs and then letting out again. Then she walked all the way back across Central London to her sweet little house on the Portobello Road, and cried again the moment she shut the door behind her.

This time, for the opposite reason.

Not because of what she'd lost.

Not because of what hurt, what was broken, what she was hiding.

But because, at last, she knew exactly who she was.

And better still, what that meant.

CHAPTER ELEVEN

ZAGO THOUGHT HE'D handled his trip to London well.

He had caught up with a few old friends, as was his usual habit. He had taken care of the usual business concerns, and had subjected himself to the usual, tedious meetings.

Notably, he did not *accidentally* find himself wandering about Notting Hill, dressed as a stranger. Though he could not claim that the notion had not occurred to him, just to see what it was like. Just to inhabit her skin a while, and get a better sense of the woman who—it turned out—haunted him with great effect even when she was only in his mind.

When he had satisfied himself that Nicolosa was well and recovering from her heartbreak, even intended to go back to university in the fall, he took himself home again.

And every time he left Venice, returning to this magical city where his ancestors had lived for some thousand years, it always reminded him exactly who he was.

Because it wasn't simply that it was heart-stoppingly beautiful to arrive in the evening and take a boat into Venice at night, though it was. It wasn't only that all the regal houses along the Grand Canal were lit up and lovely, with the lamplight spilling over the water and music echoing as if it was welling up directly from all the cracks in the weathered old buildings. It was more than that. It was more than pretty views and old bloodlines.

This was *recognition*, he thought. This was the love that he been raised on, for good or ill. The sense of place and belonging that felt as if it was a part of his bones and his very biology, and Zago did not intend to settle for anything less than that in his private life.

He would not.

And it wasn't that he second-guessed himself, he thought as the boat pulled up to his dock. Though he had certainly been tempted to, especially in London. It was more that he was bolstering up the decision he'd already made.

It also wasn't that he thought any love could exist without its challenges. That seemed impossible as long as humans were involved. But at the base of it all, he was certain it should feel like *this*.

Instant recognition. That feeling of homecoming. The knowledge that no matter where he went in this whole wide world, all these beautiful places filled with adventures and temptations aplenty, that he might love them in his way but he would always long to be *here*.

That there could be nothing on this earth that

would ever suit him better than this city. And this ruined old house that he had loved since before he could walk.

For better or worse, Zago had only ever had one home.

He walked slowly up the long stone path, looking up at the palazzo that stretched high into the night, gleaming with the same soft, thick light. And he was halfway to the impressive front door when he lowered his gaze and saw a figure sitting there on the wide stone steps.

He recognized her instantly.

In truth, he would recognize her anywhere. He had looked for her in London, in costume and out. He had puzzled over passing strangers, looking for the telltale line of her cheek, or the arch of her brow. Even the way she drew in a sharp breath. He had looked in all those crowds, forensically examined everyone who came into his field of vision, and he hadn't found her.

Yet somehow, it was no surprise at all to find her here.

Waiting.

He kept walking. He did not alter his pace. And Zago stopped there at the bottom step, his eyes on her.

Irinka, back again.

He was aware of the staff who moved around them, but mostly because Irinka smiled at them and nodded her head in greeting. Only when they were alone again, save the passing boats in the canal, did she look at him once more.

Zago let his gaze move over her. It was warm here, much warmer than it had been in London, but she had dressed for the humidity. Her black hair curled all around the way it had that first summer, even though she piled it on top of her head. She wore an easy sort of dress that looked as if it was fastened by two bows at her shoulders, then left to do what it would. He wondered if he would always notice everything. That her manicure was repaired and back to its former glory. That her toenails matched, the color of champagne. That she wore sandals that wrapped around her ankles.

And that she looked as if she had gotten sun somewhere. There was a hint of that sort of flush on her skin, right there across the crest of her nose where some people were given to freckle.

It was just the two of them, out here in the soft light of a warm Venice night.

He could hear opera echoing down the Grand Canal, though he could not take that as a sign of anything except the fact that this was Italy. Opera was a part of who they were. It had nothing at all to do with how blue her eyes were.

Or the fact that it was once again time to test his resolve.

"I saw you in London," Irinka said. But before he could respond, she lifted a hand. "I wasn't skulking around in costume, which I'm sure is your first thought. I can't blame you. But I was actually seeking out your sister, entirely as myself. I planned to apologize to her, but then I saw the two of you having dinner together and didn't feel I should intrude."

Zago didn't know what to say to that. How had he felt her so many different times, in so many different places, but not then? How had she been so close and him none the wiser?

It felt like a fundamental breakdown on the part of the universe.

"But I realized something as I was standing there," Irinka told him. "First, that an apology would be for me, not for her. I saw her smiling and it seemed cruel to go over there and bring the whole thing up again. It could possibly have made it worse. And right when you'd clearly made some headway." She took a breath. "And then I had asked myself why it was that I wanted to apologize to her, specifically, and not all the women who'd been broken up with in this particular way. By me."

Zago thought he could have jumped in there and answered, but he didn't. Surely he had said enough.

Irinka was frowning down at her hands.

"I've been on something of a journey, actually," she said after a moment. "I kept looking for the wounds."

She looked up and searched his face, and it took everything he had to stay as he was. Not precisely impassive, but not engaging, necessarily.

I am simply here to listen, he cautioned himself.

Irinka looked down again. "I kept thinking that if I could just find the thing that was broken in me, then everything would make sense."

He had never wanted to go to her more. But he couldn't let himself. It was almost like he wasn't *able* to move. He felt like some kind of statute, as if he had finally turned to stone and become one more part of this palazzo that would one day sink into the mud.

"I went to see the Duke." That moved in him like a physical blow, but he still didn't speak. "I talked to my mother. I thought about my lovely friends and the way we've always been with each other and *for* each other." Her chest moved as if she couldn't quite get a breath in. "Then I finally realized that I kept failing to ask myself the critical question."

Zago shifted his weight, then thrust his hands in his pockets. Because it was that or put them on her.

As much as he longed to do that, he could not. He could not allow himself to intervene in this. Whatever this was.

And he didn't dare hope.

"Finally," Irinka said quietly. "*Finally* it occurred to me to ask why it mattered what anyone told me or thought of me or called me. Because it shouldn't, unless I agreed." She smiled then, and he thought his heart might have shattered if it hadn't been broken into pieces already. "And I realized, at last, that this was what you've been trying to tell me. I don't think I deserve *any* of this. My father's name. His begrudging blood money. My gorgeous, marvelous friends. Even the clients I was able to round up to help out the agency. And you." That smile again. "I am certain that I don't deserve you, Zago."

It caused him physical pain not to say her name. Or to reach out and touch her, at last.

But all he could do was stand there and listen. And wait to see where she went.

Irinka's smile faded. "All this time, I kept thinking that if I really let you close, if I truly let you in, you'd see that there's nothing there. My friends still think I'm mysterious. Because I am. Because fundamentally, deep inside, I've never thought that it made sense that I was the subject of all that speculation when I was little. But I was center of so much drama and I thought that meant I had to be *worthy* of it, so I made sure no one could ever find out that I'm not. That I'm just me."

She took a breath, then blew it out a bit raggedly, and he saw what looked like a gleam of moisture in her blue gaze. "I don't know how to love anyone the right way, Zago. But I want to try. And maybe there isn't a right way. Maybe there's just you and me and this thing that I've been fighting against since I first saw you at that theater." Her breath caught. "I know it doesn't make sense, that I could enjoy being naked with you so much and yet I'm terrified of being too vulnerable. But I know that once I do this, once I *really* do this, it will be like a death. There will never be this version of me again. She will be gone forever and despite everything, I have grown rather fond of her."

For a long moment, they were both quiet. There were so many things he wanted to say. Arguments he wanted to mount and facts he was dying to point out to her, but all of it was to sway her to his side.

And he'd meant what he'd told her, more than once.

He didn't want what he had to force. Or beg for.

He wanted her love freely given. He wanted her to meet him here.

"But death is only terrifying if life is," she said quietly. "Look at this marvel of a city, propped up on little more than hopes and dreams and wooden posts. A thousand years or more of stories, ghosts, secrets, memories. Floating on. Because maybe death is just the beginning."

She stood then, and Zago had to look up, but that was no hardship when it was Irinka he was looking at. She came down one step. Another.

"Zago," she said, with a kind of solemnity that made his throat ache, "I fell in love with you so fast that it terrified me."

And something must have changed on his face, because she smiled and he saw a tear form in the corner of her eye. Then trail down her cheek.

"That first summer was so overwhelming. Maybe I died then the first time, but over and over again. I told myself it was just physical. I was sure that it was toxic. Because everything I'd always been told was that sex should be light and fluffy, a happy little pastime. I wasn't prepared for *you*, Zago. For all this intensity. For not only what you did to me, but what you demanded in turn. How fully and completely you wanted me to be present, with you, right here." She shook her head. "I couldn't do it."

Irinka came down another step. "It's more true than I would like to admit that I went back to London and found new and interesting ways to reenact our breakup with all those men, my clients. I got to throw crockery. I got to flip tables. I got to rant and scream and carry on." Her gaze was wide and shadowed. "But you and I know that our real breakup was so quiet. You looking at me with all that disappointment and me sneaking out under cover of darkness, so I wouldn't have to say goodbye. So anticlimactic. So cowardly."

She came down the final step and then she stood before him, her head tipped back and her eyes on his.

He had never seen that expression on her face before. Then again, he wasn't sure that he was breathing.

"As soon as they told me that they were taking me to Venice, I knew it was you," she confessed. "And I told myself that there were practical reasons not to cause a scene, but I didn't even try. I got on that plane and I let them bring me straight here, straight to you, because I wanted that plausible deniability. If you were a kidnapper, that made me the victim. And if I did the thing that you asked and made myself a servant, that made you look like the bad guy." Her lips curved. "And Zago, I desperately wanted you to be the bad guy."

She looked as if she was going to reach out to him, but she didn't, and it felt like a new, bright grief.

"And when I left you that time, I was convinced it was so civilized. So adult, at last. I told myself all the way home that it made up for the first time. I was drawing a line underneath it, under *us*, at last." Irinka laughed at that. "But then when I got back to England, I was a disaster. Everything was gray, inside and out. So I thought that I would come back and convince you to try again, but you were having none of it. You were saying all the things that I was afraid to even look at directly. It was terrible."

She shook her head again, but there was a different light in her eyes, now. "And I think I underestimated how hard it must have been for you to turn me away, but you did it. So of course I did what I always do. I hid. But I did it in plain sight. I followed you around, like a mad woman. And you caught me anyway. And then…you kissed me like a fairy tale and walked away without looking back." Her breath sounded ragged. "You told me that I needed to believe that I could deserve you."

This time she did reach out, and she fitted her palms to his torso, carefully. As if she was checking to see if he was real. Not stone at all, but a living, breathing man who hadn't died each time she left.

A man who had been waiting a long, long time for her.

For this.

"And I don't know what it really means to truly deserve anything," Irinka told him. "But I want to be the woman you imagine that I could be. I want to see myself in the mirror the way I can see myself in your eyes. I want to love you, as much as I can and for as long as I can, and with everything I have inside of me, until it feels like the love *you* deserve. I want to figure out how you have always been so certain, and give that back to you like the gift it is."

Tears were running down her face now, and she did nothing to hide them. She went up on her toes and tipped her face back, and he could see everything.

No games. Nothing held back.

And, if he wasn't mistaken, forever in her eyes.

"Zago," she said, this woman who had stopped his heart from the first, "I want it all. I want to marry you. I want to rattle around in this palazzo and keep it floating. I want to have your babies. Maybe a lot of them. And I want to love them all in ways that they will recognize, so they'll know, their whole lives, that no matter what else happens…they are loved. And I want to love you the same way, but more. I want to give you everything. I never want to make you wonder, ever again, that this is anything but meant to be. You, me, and no more masks." She considered for a moment, then smiled. "Except, perhaps, at Carnival."

Finally, then, Zago moved. He pulled her deeper into his arms and then his hands found her face, cradling her head in his palms while he rubbed his thumbs beneath her eyes to pick up all that moisture.

And once again, there were so many things *right there* on his lips. Vows he would make. Promises he intended to keep. Declarations and opera and all that poetry he only seemed to have inside him where she was concerned.

But what he said was simple. "What took you so long?"

And his beautiful, magical Irinka threaded her arms around his neck. She went up higher on her tiptoes and pressed her body to his, and it wasn't that he didn't feel that instant chemistry, that wildfire implosion. He knew she did, too.

But he understood when she pushed into him that what she wanted was simply to feel the way they fit together. That sweet, impossible perfection that had haunted them both all these years.

Because that was how he felt, too.

She smiled at him, ear to ear and her blue eyes sparkling. "Don't worry, my love," she said, her voice husky with all of the time they'd wasted, and all of the ground they'd covered. "I plan to make up for it with a lifetime or two. If you'll have me."

"Tesoro mio," he said, as he swept her up in his arms and held her there, like a fairy tale that would end the right way, this time. "I have only been waiting for you to say the word. Our forever starts now."

And then he showed her.

CHAPTER TWELVE

It became a year or two of marriages and babies.

Each one of Irinka's friends went before her, and for a time it seemed that all four of them were moving from one blessed event to the next. There was ample opportunity not only for them to congratulate each other and enjoy each other's company, but for their formidable billionaire men to form a most unlikely friendship of their own.

Given that each and every one of them was so... intense. Each in his own way.

At one wedding or another, they all stood together in the corner and Irinka pointed out the fact that the four men were doing the same thing on the other side of the dance floor. Huddled together like a pack of wolves, each one of whom clearly considered himself the alpha—which was likely why they got along.

"It's almost as if they've become their own set of work wives," she said.

Lynna grinned. "I can't wait to tell Athan that he has *three* work husbands."

Maude smiled serenely, holding her baby to her

shoulder. "Dominic might consider it something like déjà vu."

Auggie laughed. "I informed Matias that they have no choice but to become the best of friends. But I do like the fact that they do seem to *actually* enjoy each other."

After all, they all knew by now that trying to order around men like theirs made herding cats seem like a walk in the park.

Good job they were all particularly good at that sort of thing.

His Girl Friday changed, which was perhaps inevitable. Irinka no longer performed her previous services, but that didn't mean she didn't have other skills. She did, after all, have inroads into some of the highest levels of society. They all did now, but she was the one who was most likely to sail in, armed with a smile, and drum up business.

So that was what she did.

"I've decided that I'm going to put *rainmaker* on my business cards," she told Zago one night in London. They had decided to keep her little house on the Portobello Road. She had taken a great deal of delight in showing him around, presenting him with all the different pieces that she'd collected, and watching him study each one as if it was a window into her soul.

Maybe she hadn't appreciated the view because she'd been on the wrong side of it.

"Rainmaker?" Zago asked lazily, stroking her hair

as they sat together on her rooftop. "Because something like *client acquisition specialist* is too boring?"

"I'm happy to be anything, my love," she told him. "Except boring."

This she had proved already, deciding that it wasn't only Carnival where she could experiment with her love of costumes, but their bedroom.

He had yet to complain.

She put off introducing Zago to Roksana for as long as she could. When she finally made everyone sit down around a dinner table in her cozy house, where she could contain any damage, she was surprised to find that her mother was apparently capable of being charming when she wished.

"I had no idea you could have an entire conversation with a man without mentioning death or dismemberment," she muttered at her mother when she walked her out later. "Where has this charmer been hiding?"

"You do not think that I have had so many lovers because I cannot *charm* them, do you?" her mother replied, arching a smug sort of brow. "Silly girl."

As for their own shining, happy forever, Irinka and Zago took their time.

Nicolosa finished with university and got her first, appropriate boyfriend, who doted on her and treated her like a princess she was.

Neither Zago nor Irinka thought it wise or necessary to tell her the identity of that woman who had happily removed her from Felipe De Osma's clutches.

And while all of Irinka's friends were settling down to marriage and motherhood, she and Zago made up for lost time. He showed her the boundlessness of true love. She showed him the parts of her she had never showed anyone else, ever.

Together, they experimented with the very outer limits of vulnerability, and love, and everything in between.

When she had the urge to run away, she learned how to run to him, instead.

And when his ghosts became too much for him, she reminded him what it was like to be alive.

Irinka thought that she would have been perfectly happy to go on like this for some time. A forever or two, in fact.

So it was not until she was six months' pregnant with their first child, and quite obviously so, that Zago took her out to the balcony that looked out over the Grand Canal at another summer sunset. And as the most golden, glorious light poured over her, and him, he went down on one knee.

He looked up at her, and said, "*Tesoro mio, amore della mia vita*, I am afraid it is time."

"Already?" Irinka smiled down at him. She reached her hand down so she could hold his beloved jaw and move her thumb over his cheekbone, because it turned out she could delight in that, too. That imprinting. That muscle memory. "I was thinking we could live in glorious sin for at least the first three children."

"I would live with you in sin in a thousand lifetimes," he told her, and leaned forward to kiss her rounded belly. "But in this one, I am a Baldissera, and there are legacies to consider. And so I must beg of you, my heart and my soul and my life, to make an honest man out of me after all."

"Well," Irinka said with a sigh. "When you put it that way, how could I refuse?"

And her heart was catapulting around in her chest, but there was a lot more room in there than there had used to be. She did not hold on to age-old sobs for a lifetime, not anymore. She laughed more. She cried more.

Sometimes she shouted out her feelings without thinking them through.

Sometimes her brain got in the way of her heart, but they had found delightful ways to untangle them.

And no matter what happened, every time she reached over, Zago's hand was there to hold hers.

They were there to hold each other.

So she watched as he pulled out a ring that she had seen in the austere portraits in this grand old house. A huge diamond that she did not have to ask to know had belonged to a great many women who had lived right here, in this ancient place, surrounded not only by history but also by the history they would make.

"Will you marry me, my beloved?" Zago asked. "At last?"

"I will," she told him, and it was the easiest vow she'd ever made. "I love you so much, it almost seems as if being your wife will be too much joy to handle."

She leaned down and kissed him. "But somehow I think I will rise to the occasion."

And she did.

Thus, one day not far from then, Irinka Scott-Day gave up the name she'd kept her whole life out of spite, and took up a far better one for love, instead.

And then kept it, and cherished it—and the husband and children that came with it—all the days of her life.

* * * * *

Did you fall head over heels for
Kidnapped for His Revenge?
Then you're sure to adore the other installments in the Work Wives to Billionaires' Wives miniseries

Billionaire's Bride Bargain *by Millie Adams*
Boss's Heir Demand *by Jackie Ashenden*
The Bride Wore Revenge *by Lorraine Hall*

And don't miss these dazzling stories from Caitlin Crews!

Pregnant Princess Bride
Forbidden Royal Vows
Greek's Christmas Heir
Greek's Enemy Bride
Carrying a Sicilian Secret

Available now!